CAT-ASTROPHE?

Dmitri the cat came barreling into the room and dived under my Scarlett O'Hara hoopskirt. His tail was even bushier than my friend Wynnell's brows.

"Something's obviously spooked him." I looked around for a hard, heavy object. I picked up a trumpeting elephant with its foot raised to crush a lion. "Come on, let's go check it out."

"Abby, don't you have a burglar alarm?"

"I do. He's hiding under my skirt now."

We hadn't gone but twenty feet when I stopped abruptly. Wynnell, for whom grace is not a virtue, plowed into me. "Abby, what is it?" she hissed.

"I just remembered that I have a machete under my bed. Be a doll, dear, and get it for me. Here, take this." I thrust the heavy bookend at her.

While Wynnell went off, Dmitri lashed me repeatedly with his tail. I could tell by his fervor that he was no longer frightened but hungry. Leave it to a male to be scared silly one second, and ravenous the next.

A low cry from reverie. I started, from a deep sleep.

"Wynnell? Wha

Her response wa

D1041896

Other Den of Antiquity Mysteries by
Tamar Myers
from Avon Books

TAMAR MYERS

NIGHTMARE IN SHINING ARMOR

A DEN OF ANTIQUITY MYSTERY

AVON BOOKS
An Imprint of HarperCollinsPublishers

AVON BOOKS
An Imprint of HarperCollins*Publishers*
10 East 53rd Street
New York, New York 10022-5299

First Avon Books paperback printing: August 2001

Avon Trademark Reg. U.S. Pat. Off. and in Other Countries, Marca Registrada, Hecho en U.S.A.
HarperCollins ® is a trademark of HarperCollins Publishers Inc.

Printed in the U.S.A.

10 9 8 7 6 5 4 3 2

In memory of my father,
whose imagination was boundless.

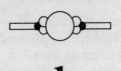

1

It isn't every day that a headless woman rings my doorbell. You can be sure, therefore, that I examined this one closely. She was about five feet, six inches tall, sans head, which she held in her right hand. Her severed neck was abnormally large, especially considering the fact that there was a bit of it still attached to her noggin. I peered harder. Yup, there were two eyeholes about five inches down.

"Wynnell!" I cried delightedly. "I'm so glad you're early. I can use all the help I can get. The caterer got sick at the last minute, and although I have all the food, it needs assembling."

The bloody stump blinked. "How did you know it was me?"

"Because you're my best friend. I'd recognize you no matter what you wore." It would not have been kind of me to mention that it was Wynnell's bushy eyebrows poking through the vision slits that had tipped me off.

My buddy sighed and stepped over the threshold. Then, really seeing me for the first time, she gasped.

1

"Abby! How did you do it?"

"Do what?" I said with a coy smile.

"You're a foot taller. At least!"

"Am I?" I smoothed a portion of my antebellum skirt, which, suspended as it was by hoops and crinolines, puffed in all directions like an organza igloo. Incidentally, I wasn't alone under all that material. My yellow tomcat, Dmitri, had been tickling my ankles with his tail ever since I'd gotten dressed.

"Abby, tell me, or I'm going to peek."

"No need," I said and hoisted my hemline.

Dmitri took one look at my headless visitor, hissed, and shot out of the room like there was a pack of dogs in pursuit.

Wynnell laughed and peered more closely. *"Stilts?"*

"Greg made them. I've been practicing all week."

Perhaps I should explain that I am normally only four feet, nine inches tall. My fiancé, Greg, is just over six feet. We would have made an odd Scarlett and Rhett without my wooden appendages. This not to say we make an odd couple in real life, but you know what I mean. Besides, if the hooped skirt gave me the opportunity to experience the rarefied strata to which the rest of you folks are accustomed, why not go for it?

"How do you manage to keep your balance?" Wynnell asked, as she bumped against the hall console.

"I don't always," I said, remembering my

bruised right knee. "I can balance about as well as you can see. But I can't walk at all in this dress without the stilts, so I'm stuck until the party's over. You, however, are another story. Why don't set your head down on that console, take off your mask, and help me in the kitchen?"

"Be glad to." Wynnell whipped off her rubber neck. "You'd be surprised how hot it is under here."

I patted my voluminous skirt. "Fifteen yards of fabric is no cool breeze."

Wynnell nodded. Her hair was damp with dew—we Southern women do *not* sweat—and her face the color of a radish.

"So what do you want me to do first?"

"Stir the punch. And taste the bowl on the left to see if it needs more pizzazz."

"Champagne?"

"Vodka. I want this party to rock."

"Abby, you're so bad. What will your mama say?"

"She gave me the recipe."

"Speaking of her, did you find out what she plans to wear tonight?"

I shook my head. "Her lips are sealed tighter than a clam at low tide. All she would say is that I was in for a big surprise."

Wynnell frowned, her damp brows fusing like giant spiders. "Doesn't that make you nervous?"

"You bet it does. Last year she came as Mother Teresa—but that was during her nun craze."

Wynnell, having tasted the bowl of spiked

punch, decided it need an extra wallop. She added enough imported spirits to keep Kiev humming for a month. And this from a Baptist!

"What does she want to be now?"

"A jockey."

"A disc jockey?"

"The kind that ride horses. Her goal is to win the Kentucky Derby before her eightieth birthday."

"Which is how far away?" Wynnell asked cagily. We Southern women would rather sweat than reveal our ages.

"She's seventy-eight."

"Then she could make it. I wouldn't put anything past your mama."

"Me, either!" I wailed. "That's just what I'm afraid of. She's liable to show up tonight at my Halloween party dressed as a jockey. A woman her age shouldn't wear those tight pants if you ask me."

"Your mama's in good shape, Abby."

"I know." I clomped over to my new oven to take a peek at the lasagna. It was ready to come out. "But she's so embarrassing. If I know her, she'll bring a real jockey with her as her date. Then who knows what the two of them will do. At least last year, when she was a nun, that wasn't a problem."

"That's only because the priest she brought with her was gay. At any rate, you're lucky to have her, Abby. Both my parents are dead."

"I know," I mumbled, "I'm a very lucky woman. I've been telling myself that all day."

And I was a very lucky woman. I, Abigail Louise Timberlake, had not only survived my divorce

from Buford the Timber Snake, but I was now engaged to Greg Washburn, the sexiest detective on
the Charlotte police force, if not the sexiest man in
the entire city. My business, the Den of Antiquity,
was doing gangbusters, allowing me to buy a
brand-new home in the exclusive neighborhood of
Piper Glen. What's more, my relationship with my
two adult children had recently progressed from
one of foe to one of friend.

"What was that, Abby? I couldn't hear you."

"Maybe that's because your ears are in the other
room."

"Good one, Abby, but seriously, what did you
say?"

"I've got this bad feeling," I said.

"About?" Wynnell took a long draft from her
punch cup. At that rate, there would be none left
for the other guests.

"About tonight."

"You're not talking about your mama now, are
you?"

A cold chill ran up my corseted spine. "What
makes you say that?"

"I didn't want to say anything, Abby, but I feel it,
too."

2

"Y ou *do?*"

My friend nodded. "I'm not claiming to be psychic—we Baptists don't go in for that—but I've been feeling really spooky about tonight."

"Spooky?" That wasn't a Wynnell sort of word.

She nodded again, this time dribbling punch down her chin. "I have this scared feeling I haven't felt since I was a kid. I almost didn't wear my costume; it was starting to really freak me out. Even at the last minute I was trying to think of something a little less gruesome. But I'd already rented this, and then when Ed said I should just stay home and watch TV with him—well, of course that left me no choice."

"Of course," I said through clenched teeth. Ed Crawford, Wynnell's husband of over thirty years, is the original stick-in-the-mud. His idea of a party is a remote control for each hand. As usual, I'd invited Ed, and as usual, he'd turned me down.

"But," Wynnell said, holding what was left of

her punch aloft, as if to make a toast, "I'm here. Let the good times begin."

My new doorbell has a lovely chime, but when it rang just then, I jumped.

"Abby, you all right?"

"Yeah, just startled. Quick! Grab your head."

I clomped, and Wynnell bumped, to the front door. I peered through the peephole first, and then flung it wide open, laughing. My dear friends, Rob Goldburg and Bob Steuben, had dressed as James Brolin and Barbra Streisand, respectively. Rob is tall and handsome and looks a bit like James anyway, but Bob's basso profundo was nothing like Streisand's voice. Still, Bob is a slight man with a prominent proboscis. Somehow he had managed to find just the right wig, and his resemblance to the megastar was uncanny.

The men seemed just as delighted by my appearance. "Oh Abby," Bob said, "now that you've finally grown, can I have your hand-me-downs?"

"If you promise to sing for us tonight."

"He fully intends to," Rob said, and looked adoringly at his life-partner.

"Sing 'Evergreen,' " Wynnell said.

James and Babs noticed the headless woman for the first time and gasped. Their reaction seemed to fluster, rather than please, Wynnell. She quickly complimented them on their costumes, then staggered off to the kitchen to fine-tune the punch.

"Is she okay?" Rob asked. His concern was genuine. The four of us worked closely in the business

together. The Rob-Bobs, as I like to call them, own
the Finer Things, which is right next to my shop.
Wynnell's store, Wooden Wonders, is directly
across the street.

"She's fine. For some reason we're both feeling
spooked today. You know that saying about a
goose walking over your grave? I feel as if there's
an entire flock up there, just gabbling away."

"Well, cut that out," Bob said jovially. "This is
your big night. This party is your chance to—"

"Speak of the goose," Rob hissed softly. "Mother
Goose, I mean."

Thanks to my new height, I could look past my
friends. Little Bo Peep was flouncing merrily up
the walk, a live sheep in tow.

"Oh Lordy," I moaned. "It's the Tweetie Bird. I
know I invited her, but I really didn't expect her to
show up. Not with Buford out of town."

Rob put a comforting hand on my shoulder. "It's
a brave woman who invites her ex and his wife,
even if she doesn't mean it. You can handle this."

I didn't have a choice, did I? I couldn't very well
renege on my invitation at this point. And yes, I
know I shouldn't have invited my ex-husband Buford and his wife, Tweetie, but at the time—and I
truly believe this—my motives were pure. I
wanted to extend an olive branch, if not for my
own personal growth, then for the sake of our children. Besides, I felt a certain kinship with Tweetie.
Sure, she had wronged me by sleeping with my
husband, but now that she'd been his wife for several years, we were both victims. The door to Bu-

ford's barn, as Tweetie so crudely put it, was never closed.

Relying on tips garnered from a college drama class, I arranged my features in a smile. "Howdy-ho, Bo. You too, Mr. Sheep."

"Abby! Is that you?"

"As big as life—well, in this case, even bigger."

Tweetie tossed her fake blond ringlets. "You look really great. How did you do it? Was it that stretching machine they've been advertising on TV lately? If it was, you might want to try their breast-inflator pump, too. I hear it really works."

"Is that so?" I said, and bit my tongue. Tweetie's breasts had been enlarged several times, but not by a pump. I know this because Buford had paid for at least one of the increments in size. The bill, you see, had first come to me by mistake.

"Of course there's no crime in being flat-chested." Tweetie thrust her manmade mammae forward like twin battering rams and prepared to enter my house.

I stepped aside. "Come on in, but the sheep stays out there."

That stopped Little Bo Peep dead in her tracks. "I can't leave her outside, Abby."

"Sure, you can. Just tie her to that tree in the backyard. There's plenty grass, and it isn't at all cold tonight."

"Yes, but what if somebody steals her? She's not mine, you know. I had to pay a hundred dollars just to rent the thing."

I tried not to laugh. "Nobody's going to steal

your sheep, dear. This is Piper Glen, not Montana."

Tweetie pursed her lips. "Well, maybe you're right. But the man said if anything happened to her I'd have to pay him another hundred dollars."

Behind me Babs, AKA Bob, gasped. He's a gourmand, and no doubt he was thinking about how many mutton chops he could get for a two-hundred-dollar investment.

Rob read my mind and nudged me. "And when we get tired of kabobs we can always eat fish."

I looked beyond Tweetie to the street. A shiny black limo was parked beside the curb, and a young man dressed as Neptune had just emerged. I watched, along with the others, in envious awe as the muscle-bound God of the Sea reached in and lifted out a mermaid with a glittering silver tail. Holding her close to his bulging pectorals he started toward us across the lawn.

"What does she have that I don't?" Bob moaned.

"Big bucks," I said. "That's Lynne Meredith."

"*Who*?"

"Major antique collector from Ohio. Moved down last month. She's got to be in her fifties; but he doesn't look a day over twenty."

Rob recoiled in mock horror. "You invited a Yankee? Wait until Wynnell hears about this."

"She knows," I said. It hadn't been easy telling my best friend that I'd invited a woman "from up the road a piece." Wynnell, although a quarter Yankee herself, is decidedly prejudiced against folks above the Mason-Dixon line. If she had it her way, there would be a barbed wire fence along the entire border. I have tried repeatedly to convince the woman that there are indeed some good Yankees—Matt Lauer, for one—but to no avail.

"Who's the stud?" Rob asked. Despite their commitment to each other, both men had their tongues hanging out like hounds after a hunt. I couldn't blame them. Tweetie and I were mesmerized by Neptune as well. Even the sheep appeared to be salivating.

I shrugged. I'd heard rumors that Lynne Meredith had a boy toy—a gigolo, if you want to be crude about it—in her employ. Apparently the rumors were true. Face it, Lynne is a plain woman with a bland personality. Vanilla yogurt is how I would describe her. And, while not substantially overweight, she has no discernible waist; hers was not the kind of midriff you wanted to see bare. It just didn't seem possible that a good looking hunk like Neptune would be in the picture unless financial remuneration was involved.

"I'll find out and fill you in later," I said. "Now be dears and go help Wynnell with the food."

James and Babs obediently headed for the kitchen. Tweetie would have followed, but I stopped her gently.

"Like I said, *you* can come in, but not the ewe."

A fake blond, Tweetie has trouble putting M&M's in alphabetical order. "You're not making any sense, Abby."

"Lose the sheep."

"All right! But if it gets stolen, you're going to pay for it." She flounced back down the steps, her woolly companion in tow. Despite her agitated state, she managed to brush up against Neptune, while somehow avoiding the mermaid's enormous tail.

I wasn't so lucky; I got a fin in my face while greeting the amphibious pair. But I learned that the stud muffin was Lynne Meredith's tennis instructor Roderick, who also happened to be from Ohio. With two Yankees at my party Wynnell was going to have a stroke. So be it. Lynne was filling up an enormous Myers Park home with antiques, most purchased from my shop. Besides, surely I could coax Lynne into buying *something* from Wooden Wonders.

The wolf whistle I heard as I showed the fishy couple in was all I needed to let me know that my Rhett had arrived. A minute later he swept me off my feet, and I mean that literally.

"My stilts!" I gasped. "Put me back down!"

Greg laughed. "Sorry about that. I got carried away there and forgot."

He held me aloft while I felt for straps with my stocking covered toes. "You're a knockout, Abby, you know that?"

Greg is tall, without stilts, and has eyes like sunlit sapphires. "Thanks, dear. You're not so bad-looking yourself. But are you saying I'm more attractive now just because I'm taller?"

"No, it's just that—well—it's a guy thing, I guess."

"So it is true? You'd prefer a taller woman! In that case, why did you make my stilts only a foot high? Why didn't you build six-foot stilts? Then I'd *really* be a tall woman."

Greg laughed and then smothered my protests with a kiss. "What I meant," he said, replacing his lips with a quieting finger, "is that guys—some guys, at any rate—find change interesting."

Some women undoubtedly found change stimulating as well. Greg's little Rhett Butler mustache, while obviously artificial, made his already scrumptious face more inviting. Were it not for my hostess duties, I'd have whisked him upstairs.

As if sensing my mood, Greg kissed me again. We might well have gone with the wind, had not my guests begun to arrive with regularity.

Geppetto and Pinocchio turned out to be Donald Larkin and his diminutive wife, Regina. They are Yankees as well, but have lived in the south so long even Wynnell forgets their distasteful origin. Another hundred years and three generations later and Larkin descendants might actually be included in Cotillion.

Moses, with his tablets of etched Styrofoam, was by day an interior decorator. Alan Bills is originally from Charleston, South Carolina, and as Southern as shrimp and grits. Alan does not plan to have descendants, so Cotillion is not an issue for him. Besides, he had his own coming-out party.

The real Statue of Liberty might be located in New York Harbor, but like Alan Bills, the woman with the flaming torch was Dixie born and bred. The fact that Irene Cheng was of Chinese ancestry did not, even in Wynnell's eyes, diminish her claim to the region.

Irene is my assistant at the Den of Antiquity and one of the most capable women I know. She does, alas, suffer from an occasional lapse of judgment.

"Irene, dear," I said gently, "put that flame out before you come in."

"Can't I at least make my entrance first?"

"No."

"Man, you're no fun!"

"I'm a ball, dear, but I refuse to have my new house burned to the ground."

Irene grudgingly extinguished the flame. "My better half couldn't make it," she said. "Had to work the night shift. Is your mama here yet?"

"Not that I know of."

"What does that mean?"

I ushered the saucy statue inside. "I've figured out who most of these folks are, but not *all* of them. See that pair of dice there? The smaller one could be Mama. On the other hand, you know my mother would never go anywhere without her pearls clearly visible, and Miss Snake Eyes over there doesn't appear to be wearing any.

"Now, that knight in shining armor could be male or female. People were a lot shorter in those days, you know."

"*Your* height?"

I gave Irene the evil eye she deserved. "Even the men were just a little over five feet tall."

"So you think that could be your mother?"

"No. Mama's five foot even and the person in that suit—"

My voice was drowned out by the gasps of my guests. In fact so much oxygen was depleted in that moment that I began to feel light-headed.

"Abby, look!" I heard Irene say. She sounded like she was in another room.

I looked, and then willed my eyes to not see what they quite obviously saw. Mama had finally arrived.

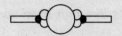

3

There was a white stallion in my foyer. It wasn't a real horse, of course, but two people in a very realistic costume. Astride the magnificent beast sat Lady Godiva—wearing nothing by yards of synthetic hair, and *pearls*!

I tottered breathlessly over to the threesome. "Mama?"

My petite progenitress smiled proudly. "Do you like it?"

"Mama!"

"That's my name, dear. Please don't wear it out."

"Mama, how could you!"

"How could I what, dear?"

"You're naked!"

"No, she's not," the horse's head said. "Look closer, Abby. She's wearing a body stocking."

I scrutinized Mama. She was indeed covered, but the fabric matched her skin tone perfectly. It was almost the same texture. Were it not for the fact that she was now anatomically incorrect, I wouldn't have believed my eyes.

16

I breathed a huge sigh of relief and turned my attention to the talking stallion. "C. J., is that you in there?"

"I didn't say anything, Abby."

"C. J., it is you! Fess up!"

The horse shook its head and pawed at my parquet floor with an oversize hoof. It was C. J., all right. No other woman I know has feet that large.

"C. J., I know you're the horse's front half, but who's his patooty?"

"That's Sergeant Bowater, Abby. You know, the guy I've been dating."

"Aha, so it is you!"

"Abby!" Mama said sharply. "Leave the girl alone!"

"Okay, okay. Sorry, C. J."

The horse nodded. I couldn't help but smile. Even though Jane Cox, AKA Calamity Jane, and therefore nicknamed C. J., is a pickle or two short of a barrel, this isn't to say the woman is mentally challenged. She is in fact a brilliant businesswoman who, at the tender age of twenty-three, started up her own antique shop, and now, a mere two years later, nets nearly as much as I do.

Mama gave me a disapproving look and then tapped the rear of her steed with a genuine riding crop. Sergeant Bowater swore softly.

"Straight ahead," Mama said. "There's room for us over by the fireplace. But mind your tail."

"Not so fast, ma mere—and her mare." I laughed at my little joke. "You don't get away from me that easy."

"Giddyap!" Mama gave the sergeant a fairly good whack.

"Damn, Mrs. Wiggins, that hurt."

I snatched the crop from Mama and grabbed her by an arm. "Mama, you're seventy-eight, for crying out loud. You sure you want to make a spectacle of yourself?"

"Absolutely. When you get to be my age, you're beyond caring what people think."

"You go, girl," C. J. grunted.

I gave my pal a gentle kick in the fetlock. "Stay out of this. But, Mama, everyone's staring."

"Sure they're staring. But that's because you're making a scene, dear."

"*Me?* I'm not the one in a flesh-colored body suit."

"Which, you must admit is very flattering— considering my advanced age."

"But it isn't you! You're supposed to wear full-circle skirts puffed out with crinolines. That's all you've ever worn since the day Daddy died—well, except for your brief stint as a novice in that Cincinnati convent."

"Oh, I wore them then, too. That's one of the reasons they asked me to leave. That and the fact I wore curlers under my wimple. But I didn't whistle on the stairs and I was never late to chapel. Those were totally trumped-up charges."

I sighed. "Okay then, make a fool of yourself. But don't blame me if my friends laugh at you. Or even worse, if a photo of you shows up in the *Char-*

lotte Observer. The paper said they might send someone over, and for all I know, they could be here right now."

Mama straightened in her papier-mâché saddle and tossed her head vainly. The heavy gold tresses remained relatively still, but a stray strand whipped me soundly across the mouth. I sputtered with surprise and indignation.

"Giddyap!" Mama barked.

The white steed moved with surprising grace and was soon swallowed by the crowd of admirers.

I sought refuge in the kitchen. The Rob-Bobs— well, Bob, at any rate—were doing a bang-up job of keeping both food and beverages flowing. I was grateful for their help considering that by then Wynnell was not only in her cups, but was in the punch bowl as well. I mean that literally.

Rob lifted her head gently out of the well-drained bowl. "She's dead drunk. Do you know what's wrong, Abby?"

"I haven't the slightest. It isn't like her at all."

"It's Ed," Bob said. He had opened a jar of cheap, supermarket-variety caviar I keep in the pantry and was deftly mixing it with the expensive but minuscule amount the caterer had supplied.

"Ed?"

"Haven't you heard, Abby? Ed's been seeing another woman."

"*What?*"

"Shhh," Rob said, as he picked Wynnell up and

cradled her in his James Brolin–like arms. "We'll fill you in later. In the meantime, where shall I put her?"

I led him upstairs to my best guest room. Believe me, it is no small feat climbing stairs in stilts, but I'd been practicing for weeks and was really quite good if I took my time. By the time we got to the guest wing, Wynnell was sawing logs like an Oregon lumberjack. Rob removed Wynnell's shoes and then looked discreetly away while I slipped that horrible costume over her head and wrapped her in a fresh terry robe. Together we tucked an antique Amish quilt around our friend.

As I closed the door behind us, I turned to Rob. "Now tell me about Wynnell."

"I'm surprised you didn't know, Abby. That's why I asked. Wynnell's been over to the shop every day—several times a day—for the last week or so. A couple of times she's even called us at home."

I almost slapped myself off those silly stilts. "But I don't understand! Wynnell's my best friend. My *very* best friend. We share everything. I can't believe I didn't have a clue."

Although my hoops contrived to keep us apart, Rob did his best to lay a comforting arm around my shoulder. He's in his early fifties and, when not made up to look like James, has thick dark hair just starting to turn at the temples. Were it not for Greg, and the small fact that Rob prefers Bob to Babs, I'd be tempted to throw myself at him.

"I think she didn't want to rain on your parade."

"What parade? You mean the clowns down-stairs?"

"It was more than just your party she was worried about spoiling. She didn't want to make you feel sorry for her—now that things are going so well between you and Greg."

"Damn that woman!" I said and stomped a foot. Unfortunately my petite pointed pump pulled loose from its strap and slipped off its perch. I teetered for a second, but despite a frantic flailing of my arms, I failed to fly. Rob caught me just in time.

"I didn't mean to do it. Honest."

Rob laughed. "Whoopsy daisy," he said, as he propped me back up.

"Thank you, Mr. Grant—I mean Mr. Brolin."

"You're welcome, Miss O'Hara."

"Would you be a gentleman, Mr. Brolin, and tighten my foot strap?"

"I'd be delighted too."

I hoisted my hoops. There is a trick to it, but I'd been practicing that as well. Suffice it to say, one tries to avoid the ladies' room, although even that is manageable. I've been to Civil War (Wynnell calls it the War of Northern Aggression) reenactments and seen ladies in period costume enter and exit the Port-O-Johns. Clearly they have a feel for such a thing. At any rate, Rob knelt and set to work.

"Tighter, dear. Greg must think I have larger feet than I do."

Rob shook his head. "These barely count as feet. What are they? Size two?"

"Four. Would you mind tightening the other strap as well?"

"My pleasure."

"So tell me, Rob, who is this woman Ed is seeing?"

"Tweetie."

I dropped my skirts, entombing the man in metal rings and layers of crinolines and heavy taffeta. From where I stood, all I could see were the backs of his legs. Unfortunately for the two of us, at that very moment Bob came bounding up the stairs, his own skirt hiked around his knees.

"Abby, where's your garlic press—oh, my God!"

"It isn't what you think," I wailed.

"Abby, how could you!"

"I didn't do anything! I just dropped my skirts."

Meanwhile Rob was trying to fight his way out of the tangle of metal and fabric without tipping me over. I'm sure it looked much worse than it was. When Rob finally emerged his face was the color of good Merlot.

"I was tightening her shoe straps," he sputtered.

Bob put his hands on his hips. The sequined sheath dress he'd chosen was surprisingly flattering.

"Yeah, right."

"He's telling the truth, Bob. This man only has eyes for you. Besides, I'm taken."

Bob softened and offered Rob his hand. "The least you can do is get up quickly before someone else sees you. This isn't the White House, you know."

Rob jumped to his feet. "Now what were you saying about garlic?"

"Forget the garlic," I snapped. "What's this about Ed and Tweetie?"

The Rob-Bobs exchanged anxious glances.

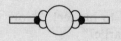

4

"**O**ut with it, you two!"

Bob cleared his throat. "I hate to be the one to tell you this but, uh, uh—"

"Tweetie's a slut," Rob said.

"And the Pope's Catholic," I said.

Four eyebrows, two of them newly plucked, raised. "You knew this?"

"I didn't know about Wynnell's husband, but of course I know about Tweetie. She slept with Buford while we were still married, didn't she? One doesn't just fall into monogamy. One works at it. And Tweetie doesn't work at anything except her hair color."

Bob made a sizzling sound. "Ouch! You sure you're not a gay man in drag, Abby?"

"Pretty sure. Look, I don't dislike the woman. I really don't. In fact, we have this weird kind of connection. She is, after all, stepmother to my children. Plus which, we've both been victimized by Buford."

"Yes, but Tweetie seems to give back to him as good as she gets."

24

"Then I say bully for her! Not that I'm condoning adultery, mind you. I'm just glad Buford finally knows what betrayal feels like from the other side of the fence."

Rob had amazement written all over his face. "You sound like you've forgiven Tweetie."

I shrugged. "I'm not sure that's the right word. Tweetie's a twit. I feel sorry for her more than anything."

Rob whistled softly. "That's more than Wynnell can say."

"Give her a chance, dear. How long has this affair been going on, and how long has Wynnell known about it?"

"Affair?" Bob boomed, in his not-so-Barbra voice. "Is that what you told her?"

Rob spread his hands. "Well—"

"It's not an affair?" I demanded.

"Apparently it was just a one-time thing. But that counts, doesn't it?"

"In my book, yes. Go on."

Rob looked triumphantly at his partner. "It happened after the Christmas party. Wynnell just found out about it."

"How?"

"Apparently Ed doesn't clean his suits very often. Now with the weather getting cooler Wynnell took a couple in and, well, you can guess what happened."

"She found a motel receipt in the pocket?"

They both nodded. "Very cliché," Bob said, "but so is the entire situation. Older man, younger woman. Pot-belly, silicone. Sounds like B-grade movie material."

I snorted. "Sound like Ed's a bit of a twit, too."

Rob cleared his throat. "Maybe—but maybe not. He may be kind of a dull man, but he's also very conscientious."

"You mean he wanted to be caught?"

"Now you're cooking with gas, Abby."

"But why? And why wait so long?"

"Permit me." Bob tugged on a bra that was obviously riding up. "Wynnell says their marriage has been flat for a long time. She thinks Ed might just be tired of her, but too chicken to ask for a divorce."

"The ironic thing," Rob said, "is that Wynnell has been unhappy, too. She was thinking about divorce as well, until she found out about Tweetie. Suddenly she's appreciating what she has, and wants to keep it."

"Doesn't make any sense," Bob said. "We think she's just afraid of being lonely."

I can't begin to tell you how hurt I was to hear the Rob-Bobs say these things. Wynnell has been my best friend for years. We share *everything*—or at least I thought we did. How could she confide in the Rob-Bobs, and not me? And speaking of friends, why didn't the guys tell me earlier that Wynnell was hurting? They tell me everything else, and often in far too great detail.

I was about to give them a piece of Scarlett's mind when the phone rang.

*   *   *

I took the call in my upstairs den. It's where I re-
treat to read a book, listen to music, and yes, even
watch television. It was in my La-Z-Boy recliner
by the phone where I watched Marian Colby lock
Adam Chandler in his Y2K shelter, and where I
tried to warn Erica Kane to stay away from that
self-involved heart surgeon.

"Abby's house of pandemonium," I said
breezily.

"Mrs. Timberlake!"

"Just a minute," I let Scarlett say. "I'll see if
she's in."

"Mrs. Timberlake, that is you speaking, isn't it?"

"Is it?" I said cagily.

"It is! And do you know who this is?"

"Do I?" I knew who it was all right. There is no
confusing Captain Keffert with anyone else. Since
he is a valued customer I try hard to think of his
brusqueness as a charming by-product of his Connecticut origins. That is certainly how I explain his
and his wife's eccentricity.

"You're darn tooting, little lady, so I'm going to
stop beating around the bush. I want to know why
you didn't invite my wife and me to your party."

"Party?"

"Darn it, Mrs. Timberlake, you're going to force
me to use stronger language."

I sighed. "Okay, so I'm having a little get-to-
gether. But it's only for a couple of close friends."

"Lynne Meredith is your friend?"

I gulped. "You know Miss Meredith?"

"We met in your shop, Mrs. Timberlake. You introduced us. Thought we might know each other because we're both from beyond the pale."

"The pale what?"

"The *pale*, as in—oh, never mind. My point is she's just another collector. Isn't that right?"

"Captain, I fail to see how this is your concern."

"It is my concern because my wife and I are big customers of yours as well, and we didn't get invited. We bought that Queen Anne period walnut secretary from you last week. The one with the Boston provenance. Didn't you joke that you could send your son to Harvard with your profits?"

"Did I say Harvard? I thought sure I said Yale."

"Mrs. Timberlake, this is no laughing matter. My wife is sitting here weeping as I speak. She's convinced her position in Charlotte society has been permanently stunted thanks to you slighting us."

I was both stunned and thrilled. I'm just a little old gal from the backwaters of Rock Hill, South Carolina. I'm a relative newcomer to Charlotte myself. I barely know the boundaries of Charlotte society, much less have set a toe in that exclusive realm. I certainly—and you can bank enough to send your child to Harvard on this—am not in a position to influence anyone else's standing in the community.

"Captain Keffert, I have not slighted anyone. And I'm sure your wife's standing in Charlotte society has not been affected."

"Ha! That's easy for you to say. You rub elbows with the elite on a daily basis, while we, just because of our transplant status, must content ourselves with the hoi polloi."

I didn't know which misconception to address first. In the end I decided not to dissuade the captain of his conviction that I hobnobbed with the crème de la crème of Charlotte society.

"Sir, I assure you that your immigrant status has little to do with your position. This is Charlotte, after all, the banking center of the southeast. All you have to do is buy your way in. It is only in Charleston—and that's in South Carolina—that you have to be born to the manor."

He seemed to cogitate on that for a moment. "How do I do that?" he finally asked. "I mean, buy my way in."

"I don't know," I said honestly. "Not having done it myself. But I can make some guesses."

"Please," he begged, "tell me what you think."

I love giving solicited advice. "I think you might consider donating a large amount to some charity. Maybe several charities. And join the right church, of course."

"Episcopal?"

"Close. Episcopal is front line in Charleston, but second line here. First line here is Presbyterian."

"Well, I guess we could manage that. Anything else?"

"Do you belong to a country club?"

"Neither of us plays golf."

"Oh dear. You're missing the point. You need someplace to eat Sunday lunch. Some place to be *seen*."

"There is a nice restaurant on the lake we've been meaning to try."

"Heavens," I said in mock horror, "that won't do at all. It can't be a public restaurant. The hoi polloi eat there."

"Mrs. Timberlake, are you making fun of me?"

"Perhaps just a little," I confessed. "Look, Captain, it's been interesting, but I really have to get back to my guests."

"Ah, your guests. Mrs. Timberlake, for my wife's sake is there any way I could get you to reconsider? You know, to expand your guest list." He started to whisper. "For a reasonable fee, of course."

I was shocked. The nerve of that man trying to buy his way to my party! Okay, so I was flattered as well, but I really couldn't accept paying customers at my party. Who knows where that trend could lead? And yes, I know, I could have just capitulated and told the couple to hustle their bustles over, and that I wouldn't charge them a farthing, but I hate being bullied.

"Captain Keffert, the answer is no, and I'm afraid this conversation is over."

"Mrs. Timberlake, I hope you realize that you just may be losing a customer."

"Is that a threat?" I snarled. I really try to mind my manners, but enough is enough.

"It's more than a threat, Mrs. Timberlake. This is the end of our doing business together—well, almost the end. The end will be Monday when I return that Queen Anne period secretary."

I gasped as he hung up the phone. I gasped again a second later when it rang a second time.

"You can just forget my next party, too!" I barked.

"Abby? Is that you? Are you all right?"

"I'm fine," I said warily.

Malcolm Biddle is Buford's junior law partner. Buford Timberlake may be as treacherous as a snake, but Malcolm is as slippery as a slug soaked in olive oil. While we were married, whenever the snake went on a business trip, he'd have the slug call me. The purpose of the call was ostensibly to check on my welfare, but I knew Buford's main concern was whether I was cheating on him. What Buford didn't know was that what Malcolm really did was hit on me.

"You don't sound fine, Abby."

"I'm just tired. It's been a long day. Is there something you want, Malcolm?"

"I hear you're having a party."

"Yes, I am. It's an absolutely delightful party and you're not invited."

"Abby, is that nice?"

"Was it nice of you to ask me to bed when I was married to your boss?"

"I think it was. Abby," he purred, "there's no reason to sleep with the rest when you can sleep with the best."

"Malcolm, this conversation is over." I started to hang up but stopped when I heard the intensity of his protest. You might think it was foolish of me to engage him in conversation again, but there was a slim chance Malcolm was charged with delivering a message from Buford. One that somehow involved our two grown children. Just for the record, you never stop being a parent.

"Abby, you still there?"

"Yes. But you have exactly three seconds."

"It's about Tweetie."

"What about her?"

"Is she there?"

"Aha! So now Buford has you checking on her. Are you going to make a pass at her as well?"

"Abby, don't be silly. She's just a little girl."

"Yeah, a twenty-four-year-old one with a forty-inch bust."

"That means nothing to me. It's a woman's brain I find sexy, and you, Abby, have a—"

"Bye-bye, Malcolm."

"Don't hang up! Just tell me if she's there."

I sighed. "Yes, she's here."

"Did she come by herself?"

"She came with a sheep."

"Excuse me?"

"This is a costume party, Malcolm. The *little girl* came as Little Bo Peep."

He laughed. "This sheep is some shaggy-haired dude, right?"

"No, it's a sheep. Baaaaaaa."

"Well, I'll be damned."

"Look, Malcolm, tell your boss his bimbo is safe and sound, and unless that sheep turns out to be a ram, she's probably chaste as well. Also tell him

that if the beast eats my camellias, I want replace-
ments."

Malcolm laughed again, but promised he'd pass
on my message. He also made a very obscene sug-
gestion. I'm pretty sure, however, that I managed
to slam the phone receiver down hard enough to
do some damage to his ear.

The party went downhill from there. C. J. and
Sergeant Bowater decided they were tired of being
Mama's white steed and preferred to be a bucking
bronco. Unfortunately Mama was still astride the
pair when they leaped into the air, but alas, not for
long. Mama was sent flying across the room, landing in Geppetto's lap. Neither of them was hurt,
but Mama became tangled in Pinocchio's strings,
and in the process of extricating herself ripped her
flesh-colored body suit. Unfortunately her faux
blond locks came just down to, but didn't cover,
her ample Wiggins bottom.

The sight of Lady Godiva's real derriere caused
the Statue of Liberty to drop her torch. Unfortunately Miss Liberty, AKA Irene Cheng, had dis-
obeyed my order, and while I was upstairs with
Wynnell and the Rob-Bobs, she'd relit her pyro-
genic prop. Although my fire-retardant carpet did
not go up in flames, it did start to smoke. Lynne
Meredith, the mermaid, was well-meaning when
she slapped the smoldering spot with her tail, but
she only succeeded in fanning the fibers into a
proper flame.

It was Moses who saved the day. He beat my

Berber with his tablets of the law, and when that failed to extinguish the fire, he dumped the bowl of nonalcoholic punch on the conflagration. This not only put out the fire, but produced a pleasingly pink stain about three feet across. Along about this time my smoke alarm finally kicked in.

Instead of frightening my guests, the smoke alarm's shrill sound sent them into paroxysms of laughter. A few incorrigibles, like Mama, tried to outshriek the device. By then I'd had it.

"Everybody out!" I screamed. "Out, out, out!"

They ignored me, although the smoke alarm eventually listened.

"Y'all can hear me now!" I screamed again. "The party is over!"

Alas, no one paid attention to the harried O'Hara.

"Greg, do something," I begged.

My fiancé didn't hear me because he was too busy singing a duet with Barbra Streisand. I turned to Rob for assistance, but he was so jealous of Greg—quite needlessly, I might add—he didn't even know I was there.

"C. J.!" I wailed. "You're my friend. Make them listen."

But C. J. was still coupled with Sergeant Bowater in the stallion costume, and obviously still quite in character. She neighed and pawed the air with a rubber hoof, which only provoked fresh peals of laughter.

I was at my wit's end. I had no choice, therefore, but to resort to drastic measures.

5

I'm not proud of what I did. But as I see it, I really had no choice. At any rate, the Charlotte police were very responsive and arrived within five minutes of my call. The second the two young officers strode into my great room, the ruckus ceased. The rumblings, however, persisted well into the night.

"I can't believe you did that, Abby!" Mama had tied one of my aprons around her waist, the skirt to the back. Strangely, she looked more provocative that way than she had with her derriere exposed.

"I warned y'all, Mama. What else could I do?"

"You could try treating your little old mama with respect." Mama flipped a strand of the coarse wig away from her face and in the process inadvertently hit me in the eye again. "Come on," she said to the others, without bothering to apologize to yours truly. "The party is reconvening at my house."

You would have thought by their responses that each of my guests had won the lottery. They flocked around Mama, cheered her, and Greg, who didn't know what was good for him, hoisted her back onto the hokey horse.

Then the crowd—and there were far more present than the aforementioned—danced out of my house in a joyous procession. As the merrymakers passed me, more than a few paused just long enough to assault my ears with vicious accusations.

"You're a real spoilsport," Moses said gravely. "I drove all the way up from Charleston and spent good money on a motel for tonight. Don't expect me to return the favor next year by inviting you to my party."

I nodded, on the verge of tears.

The Rob-Bobs, good friends that they were, didn't even notice my vulnerable state. Bob boogied past me without making eye contact, but Rob gave me a pitying look.

"This could be bad for your business, Abby," he said. "Really bad. That couple in the dice costumes are Jerry and Lizelle Wentworth."

The tears began to fall as Rob rejoined his partner in what was virtually a conga line. The Wentworths were one of the wealthiest, if not *the* wealthiest, of the many nouveau riche families the Charlotte economy had spawned in the last several years. Not having inherited any antiques from their blue-collar ancestors, the couple was buying up area antiquities like they were shares of Microsoft stock.

Mama, seeing my tears, bade her steed to halt momentarily. "Abby, your mascara is smearing.

You better fix it before you start looking like a panda bear."

"Mama! Don't you have anything comforting to say?"

Apparently she didn't, because she whacked Sergeant Bowater with her crop and the traitorous trio galloped on into the foyer.

Lynne Meredith, whose fins had fanned the fire, and who was therefore partly responsible for the debacle, had the nerve to verbally accost me next. "You've seen the last of my business," she snarled. "I can't recall the last time I've been treated so rudely. And I thought you Southerners were gracious."

"We are!" I wailed. "We just don't like having our new homes destroyed."

"Sherman had the right idea," she whispered behind a webbed hand.

I reeled with shock.

"Scrooge," Neptune said as he whisked the mean mermaid away before I could recover enough to retaliate.

"Wrong holiday!" I shouted after the aquatic duo.

The Larkins, who had lived in the South long enough to learn good manners, proved not to be apt students. Geppetto stood passively by while Pinocchio punched the air with a faux wood finger as she delivered each scathing word.

"You owe your mother an apology, Abby. I can't imagine throwing mine out of my house. For shame, for shame, for shame!"

"Does your mama show up at parties in a nude body suit?" I demanded. •

Before the pushy puppet could reply, Ireng Cheng, the woman who had started the fire, stepped between us. Her crown was askew, her book bent, and her robe smudged. Her torch, thank heavens, was still extinguished.

"Abby, do I still have my job?" It sounded more like a demand than a question.

I tried to glare at Lady Liberty, but lacked the spirit. The woman might be a menace at a costume party, and is as stubborn as a room full of two-year-olds, but she is a very competent shop assistant. If I sacked Irene, I was going to have to hustle more than I cared to, or else break in a new assistant. The latter was a prospect about as daunting as my impending marriage.

Don't get me wrong, I'm eager to wed Greg. It's just that I'm set in my ways, both at home and in my shop. And while I may be only in my late forties, I've grown accustomed to the luxury of a slower-paced life that only good help can bring. Did I really want to get up each morning in time to open the Den of Antiquity, and if I didn't, was I willing to live with the lost revenue?

"You have your job," I said through clenched jaws. "But I have half a mind to garnish your wages for the damage you did to my carpet."

Irene had the temerity to smirk. "Which you wouldn't do, of course, on account of it was not a work-related accident."

"It wasn't an *accident* of any kind," I snapped. "I

told you to put the flame out before you came in. But of course you wouldn't listen, so not only did you ruin my carpet, you ruined my party."

Irene rolled her eyes. "I didn't dump the punch on it. Moses did."

"To put out the fire *you* started!"

Irene adjusted her crown in the mirror behind me. "My, aren't we shrill."

"Shrill?" I shrieked. "Do you want to hear shrill?"

"Hey, Abby," Greg said, "take it easy."

I stared up at my intended. "I think I'm taking it very easy considering the circumstances. Heck, I'm practically comatose."

"Kicking everyone out is hardly taking it easy."

"It isn't your house that's been ruined. And you had no business encouraging Mama."

"I didn't."

"You put her back up on that silly horse, didn't you? What do you call that?"

"Abby, simmer down."

"Don't tell me what to do, Greg." There was enough ice in my voice to push the season forward by two months. Irene Cheng, along with the rest of the conga line stragglers, wisely took a clue and slipped out the door.

My fiancé spread his large hands in a gesture of mock compliance. "Hey, I'm only trying to appeal to your reasonable side."

"*My* reasonable side? If you had a shred of loyalty you would have stuck up for me. I wouldn't have had to call your buddies in blue if you'd helped tone things down a bit. But oh no, you had to belt out a Streisand tune at the top of your lungs while—"

"Abby," he said sharply, "I've had enough of this for tonight. When you're ready to discuss things calmly, give me a call. I'll be at your mother's."

"Frankly, my dear, I don't give a damn," I said and gently pushed Rhett Butler out the front door.

I didn't have the energy to clean up the mess that night. Instead I took two aspirin and—okay, so it wasn't aspirin I took, but Xanax. But it was just one very small .5mg pill. I don't normally take drugs to help me sleep, but this was, you'll have to admit, a special occasion. The medication was, by the way, left over from a small dosage prescribed by a doctor two years ago when I found a body in an armoire.

At any rate, still dressed as Scarlett I teetered in to check on Wynnell before going to bed. To my surprise, I found the room empty.

"Well, if that doesn't beat everything," I said aloud. "First Mama, then my boyfriend, and now my best friend."

"What about me?"

I whirled, and in the process lost my balance. The fancy little jig I did to stay upright was a wonder to behold.

"You scared me half to death!" I said between gasps.

"I only went to the bathroom, Abby. Say, where is everyone?"

"They, uh, they went home."

Wynnell yawned and glanced at the dresser clock. "So early? You mean I missed the entire party?"

"I'm afraid so, dear. Only you didn't miss much. It was more like a trade union protest than a party."

Wynnell sat on the bed and rubbed her head. "You mean it got rowdy?"

"You might say that. Mama came as Lady Godiva. C. J. was her horse. Take it from there."

"And the *others*?"

Perhaps I only imagined the special significance she attached to that word. But then again, perhaps not. I decided it was time to bring things out into the open. If my friend turned on me for doing so—well, maybe the Xanax would help.

"*She* came as Little Bo Peep. Even brought a live sheep with her."

The hedgerow brows raised in unison. "She who?"

"Tweetie. It's all right, dear, I know everything."

Wynnell sat silent for a moment. "I thought I could trust them," she said finally. "Apparently not."

"What about me? Do you think you can't trust me? Is that why you didn't tell me?"

Wynnell shook her head, and then grimaced at the pain it caused. "I wanted to spare you, Abby."

"Spare me what?"

She stared at me, as if willing me to read her thoughts. "You know."

"No, I don't."

"Tweetie," she said. If words were fingers, hers were holding a stranger's dirty lingerie.

"Ah. You thought that if you told me, it would stir up painful memories."

Wynnell blinked. "Does it?"

I shrugged. "Not really. It's been a while and—well, to be absolutely honest, I pity her more than anything else."

"Abby, how can you of all people say that? The woman's a—"

"A witch?"

"That's putting it politely. She's a slut and a home-wrecker too. I only hope that someday she gets what's coming to her."

"Well, it isn't Ed."

Wynnell seemed to rally. "Expound," she said.

"Ed doesn't want Tweetie—not really, and I daresay she doesn't want him."

"But then why did he sleep with her?"

"Ask him. Maybe he was feeling lonely."

Wynnell nodded slowly. "Maybe. I haven't exactly been there a lot for him lately—if you know what I mean."

"Spare me the details, please, but yes, I do know."

"That still doesn't make it right."

"Of course not. Ed's a skunk." I counted to three. "But he's still a keeper."

"You think so?"

"Definitely. It would be too much trouble to train a new husband, right?"

Wynnell laughed. "Abby, he's not a dog. He's a skunk."

"Same thing. Beside, you've been together now—how long?"

"Thirty-one years."

"You see! Think of all that shared history wasted if you two were to go your separate ways."

She studied her nails. "But you didn't forgive Buford."

"Well, at least not for a couple of years. Then I realized my hate was hurting me more than him. Anyway, it's not the same thing. Ed's dalliance with Tweetie was a onetime thing. Buford—well, he married her, didn't he?"

"So are you saying I should just turn the other cheek?"

"Not at all, dear. Thrash him soundly, within an inch of his life, if you're up to it. At the very least make him grovel. But in the end, forgive. You'll feel better for it."

"Maybe you're right."

"I know I am—and, oh, this incident should be worth at least a cruise."

"Abby, you are so bad!"

"Right again as well. Hey, you want to stay the night? It will make him worry."

Wynnell grinned. "Sure."

"I took a Xanax," I confessed, "so I might start

feeling a little draggy, but if you want, we could bring the leftover food up here and watch TV in my room. I taped *All My Children*."

"Abby, you know I don't care for soaps. Isn't there something else we could watch?"

"Well, I think there's a chick flick on Lifetime."

"That Julia Roberts movie? I've seen it twice. Abby, don't you have anything a little more *adult*?"

I thought for a moment, and then flushed. "Buford bought me a tape once. I don't know why I still have it. Anyway, he said he thought it might improve our—well, sex life. It's called *Stan Does Seattle*."

"Bingo!" Wynnell clapped her hands in glee.

I couldn't help but smile. If watching a tawdry video made her feel like she was getting back at Ed, I was all for it. Very few sexual diseases get transmitted through VCRs, and viewers almost never get pregnant.

"Okay," I said gamely. "Stan it is. Just let me get out of this costume and—"

Dmitri, whom I'd not seen since Wynnell had scared him out of his wits at the front door, came barreling into the room and dived under my skirt. His tail was even bushier than my friend's brows.

"It wasn't me who scared him this time," Wynnell said. "He didn't even look at me."

"I know, but something's obviously spooked him." I looked around for a hard, heavy object. In the old days I would have grabbed one of Buford's golf trophies. Now the best I came up with was a pair of bronze bookends. I picked up one, a trumpeting elephant with its foot raised to crush a lion. "Come on, let's go check it out."

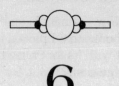

6

"Abby, don't you have a burglar alarm?"

"I do. He's hiding under my skirt now."

"That isn't funny, Abby."

"Okay, so I've put off installing a security system."

"Then don't you think we should call the police?"

"Wynnell, I don't really think there's an intruder. Dmitri acts crazy like this all the time. I'd feel better, though, taking a quick tour of the house, just to make sure all the doors and windows are locked. You coming with, or not?"

She glanced around the room. A small Tiffany lamp with a low-wattage bulb on the nightstand was the only illumination, and the room practically crawled with shadows.

"Coming."

Armed as I was, I led the way. We hadn't gone but twenty feet when I stopped abruptly. Wynnell, for whom grace is not a virtue, plowed into me. Fortunately the woman has long arms and was able to catch me before I toppled off my height enhancers.

"Abby! What is it?" she hissed.

"I just remembered that I have a machete under my bed."

"You *do*? Whatever for?"

"I bought it in Jamaica the last time I was there. It's actually an antique. It was used for chopping cane on a sugar plantation. Anyway, I was going to put it in my shop, but then decided it didn't hurt to have a weapon around the house. I'm not about to get a gun."

"We should get it!" She gave me a little push.

I waved my arms until I caught my balance. "Be a doll, dear, and get it for me. I'd have to take off my stilts just to reach under the bed. I might even have to remove my dress, if the machete has been pushed back too far."

"Oh no, you don't! You're not sending me in alone."

"My bedroom is right there," I said pointing to the nearest door. "Here, take this!" I thrust the heavy bookend at her.

She took it reluctantly. "Okay, but you're getting a burglar alarm. One that doesn't eat cat food."

While Wynnell went off to get the knife, the beast in question lashed me repeatedly with his tail. I could tell by his fervor that he was no longer frightened, but hungry. Leave it to a male to be scared silly one second and ravenous the next.

Buford was that way. Only with him it wasn't fear, but amorousness. I used to envy other women whose husbands purportedly dropped off to sleep after fulfilling their marital duties. Mine always wanted a steak dinner. One time he requested a—

A low cry from Wynnell interrupted my reverie. I started, as if suddenly awakened from a deep sleep.

"Wynnell?" I clomped toward the bedroom. "What's wrong, dear?"

Her response was an ear-splitting scream.

I twisted my right ankle in getting to her. In fact, I lost that stilt altogether. Poor Dmitri got stepped on more times than I care to remember, but somehow I managed to make it to my friend's side in a matter of seconds.

At first I could see nothing amiss. Wynnell was kneeling beside the bed, as if to get the machete, and she still had her head. Her *real* head. There didn't appear to be anyone else in the room with us—until Wynnell rocked back on her heels.

"What the heck is that?"

"Abby," Wynnell moaned. "Oh, Abby, it's awful."

I threw off the other stilt and sank into a pile of collapsed hoops beside my friend. Barely protruding from the dust ruffle was a metal helmet, but when I flipped up the bed skirt, I could see the entire suit of armor. The *same* armor I'd seen the mystery guest wearing earlier.

"Finders keepers, losers weepers," I said. It was just a costume, of course, but very convincing. It would look splendid in my new foyer. Not that I would really keep the armor, mind you—well, maybe, if the guest didn't return for it.

"But Abby, there's somebody in there."

"There *is*?" I started to lift the visor, but Wynnell grabbed my wrist.

"Trust me, you don't want to look."

"Why not?"

"He's dead."

"Dead?" I peeled her fingers loose with my free hand and opened the visor to see for myself.

Sure enough, there was a dead person in that suit of armor. And yes, it was an awful sight to behold. But Wynnell was wrong about one thing.

"This isn't a man," I said softly. "It's Tweetie."

Greg answered the phone at Mama's. "This better be Domino's Pizza, and you better be calling from just around the corner."

"Huh?

"I have a starving crowd over here. Please don't tell me you're lost again."

"Honey, it's Abby."

"Abby! Where are you?"

"At home. Greg, something—"

"Hey, you're not still sulking, are you? Because your mama's party is really rocking. You need to get on over here."

Mama's party? I'd planned the party months ahead of time, compiled the guest list, had invitations printed up, and now Lady Godiva was getting all the credit.

I swallowed my irritation. "I'm not sulking, Greg. I called to tell you that Tweetie Timberlake is dead."

"*What?* Say that again, Abby. It's kinda noisy in here. For a second I thought you said Tweetie is dead."

"She is." I practically shouted. In the background I could hear C. J. braying like a donkey while Mama sang "Don't Sit Under the Apple Tree" at the top of her lungs. When she gets in her cups, which honestly isn't all that often, my petite progenitress hauls out her repertoire of World War II songs. It was during that time period, incidentally, when she met Daddy.

"Abby, this isn't some mean-spirited joke, is it?"

"No. I wouldn't joke about a thing like this. Tweetie's been murdered."

"Hey, hold it down in there," he shouted, his hand only half-covering the receiver. He got back on. "How? Where? When?"

"I think she was strangled. And it happened here. But I don't know when—well, tonight of course."

"Strangled? What makes you think that?"

"Both her eyes and her tongue—never mind," I wailed, trying to erase that awful image from my mind. "The point is, she's dead."

"Did you call 911?"

"I'm tiny, Greg. I'm not an idiot."

"Right. Sorry. Look, just sit tight. I'll be over in a flash."

"You're at Mama's in Rock Hill," I reminded him, and not without a trace of bitterness. "It would take you twenty minutes in a squad car to get back to Charlotte. It will take you at least thirty in your own car. I could be tried and convicted by then."

"Or it could take forty minutes if we keep chatting. Bye, Abby."

I didn't have time to react. Before Greg could hang up, Mama was on the line.

"Abby, are you all right?"

I swallowed enough sarcasm to induce a bad case of indigestion. Unfortunately there was some left over.

"Yes, Mama, I'm perfectly all right. My party was ruined and now I have a dead woman in my house. Come to think of it, I'm more than all right. I'm fine as frog's hair split three ways"

"Abigail!" Mama said in a tone she hadn't used since I was a teenager. "What's going on? Why is Greg leaving?"

Mama claims she has the ability to smell trouble. She means that literally. Clearly the polyester wig and nude body suit were interfering with her sensory capabilities.

"Tweetie is dead," I said flatly. "You didn't smell *that* one coming, did you?"

There was a long pause. "I'm coming right over, Abby."

I softened. "No need, Mama. Thanks, anyway. Wynnell is here, and any minute the bell's going to ring and—"

It rang on cue.

"Gotta go, Mama. I'll call later."

7

The paramedics were the first to arrive, followed only seconds later by the men in blue. The house was swarming with people when I answered the doorbell for the umpteenth time. Had I been wearing false teeth, I would have swallowed them when I saw the dead ringer for Tweetie standing on my front porch.

The woman flashed a badge at me. "Investigator Sharp," she said in a high girlish voice. "Say, you look like you've seen a ghost."

I stared at her in disbelief. She was the spitting image of the newly deceased—well, except that Tweetie had been a bottle blond, and this woman's hair color was obviously natural. One can always tell, you know. There is more to being blond than just stripping perfectly good brown hair of its pigment. At any rate, other than the origins of their respective hair colors, they were physically identical. It was as if they had bought their faces and figures from the same plastic surgeon, using the same catalogue of silicone body parts. There was, however, something different about the look in the detective's eyes. And I'm not just talking about how it differed from the look in Tweetie's eyes when I opened that visor. *This* bimbo had an aura of cunning about her that the dead woman never had.

"Uh, uh, you look familiar."

"Do I?" She held out a manicured hand. "You're Abigail Timberlake, right?"

I frowned. There are some pretty sick people out there in the world, and a few of them happen to be my friends. Could it be possible that this was all an elaborate practical joke?

"May I see your badge, please," I said in a guarded voice.

"Certainly." She actually handed it over to me. It was every bit as heavy and appeared to be as genuine as Greg's. I memorized the number before returning it.

"You can't be too careful." I still wasn't sure the woman was telling the truth. Her striking similarity to the dead woman aside, the alleged detective wasn't dressed in a professional manner. The males I knew in the department generally wore khaki slacks and navy blazers. Neckties were de rigueur. The woman identifying herself as Investigator Barbara Sharp was wearing a black velvet dress that fell far short of her knees. It didn't do such a good job of covering her bosom, either.

"You're right about that. May I come in?" She sailed past me without waiting for an answer.

"Hey!"

"That's all right, Abby." I felt Greg's hand on my shoulder. "Let her go. She has a job to do."

I turned and threw myself into the arms of the man I loved. When all was said and done, what did it matter if he'd deserted me to make merry with Mama and her minions? He was here now that I needed him. That's what really mattered.

"You holding up okay?" he asked. Genuine concern was registering in those brilliant blue eyes.

"I'm okay—well, I guess I'm really not. This all seems so unreal."

He squeezed me gently. "You're in shock. That's only natural. Did you tell the kids yet?"

"No."

"Would you like me to tell them?"

I shook my head. Both Susan and Charlie would still be up. Neither of them had been close to their stepmother, and while telling them would be awkward, sad even, it was certainly manageable. Telling my ex-husband was another story. *That* could go either way. Depending on the mood he was in, Buford might well burst into tears over the phone, or he could just as easily launch into an angry diatribe, accusing me of killing Tweetie.

"Has anyone called Buford?"

"I don't know. I gave his number to one of the uniformed officers."

Greg kissed me. "You call the kids, while I check on things. If nobody's called Buford, I will."

"Thanks, dear."

While my real-life knight, who owns no armor, charged off to gather information, I called the kids from the phone in my den. First Susan, who was enjoying a semester abroad in a small village in southern France, and then Charlie. I was surprised to get Susan so easily.

"You want me to come home, Mama?" she asked. My daughter prides herself on her acting ability, but I could see right through her.

"There wouldn't be much point to it, would there, dear? I mean, she'll probably be buried by the time you could get here. Anyway, don't you have midterms or something coming up?"

"Yeah, right," Susan said, jumping too easily at my manufactured excuse. My daughter, I knew, despised the woman who'd torn her family apart.

My son, Charlie, who attends Winthrop University in Rock Hill, was not particularly saddened, either. He volunteered to come and spend the night with me, but I could tell by his voice that he wasn't keen on sleeping in a house where a corpse had just been discovered. I graciously turned him down.

I had no sooner hung up when Greg came into the room with Wynnell and Investigator Sharp in tow. I did another double take.

"How did it go?" he asked.

"As well as can be expected. They're upset, of course"—I decided to be utterly honest—"but they're not heartbroken."

Greg nodded. "Abby, the investigator would like to ask you a few questions."

"Now?"

Investigator Sharp stepped forward. "Yes, Mrs. Timberlake. It's routine in situations where foul play may have been involved."

"*May* have been involved? Look, Tweetie was definitely murdered."

"Well, that is for forensics to determine, isn't it? Until we get the coroner's report—"

"Tweetie did not kill herself," I said through gritted teeth. "She certainly didn't stuff her own corpse in that suit of armor and shove it under my bed."

"Hey Abby, simmer down," Greg whispered.

"I will not!" Nothing makes me want to pipe up like being told to simmer down.

Investigator Sharp was sporting a smirk. Greg may not have seen it, but I'm sure Wynnell did.

"Mrs. Timberlake, I was hoping you'd be more cooperative."

"I'm very cooperative," I snapped. "But I'm not the only one you should be interviewing. Why start with me?"

That surprised her. "Who else was here all evening?"

"My friend Wynnell Crawford here. She found the body."

Wynnell scowled behind fused brows. "You sent me into that room, Abby."

The investigator looked Wynnell over, and apparently deciding she looked harmless, turned back to me. "Mrs. Timberlake, it was your party. I prefer to start with you."

Greg poked me in the side with a long tan finger. "Cooperate," he said just above a whisper.

"Do I have a choice?" Mama probably heard my whisper all the way down in Rock Hill.

Investigator Sharp surprised me by laughing. "You're feisty. I like that. And since you're being blunt, I'll return the favor. You could refuse to talk, but that wouldn't look good for you. You could ask Greg to stay, but that wouldn't look good for him. I'm the one who's been assigned to this case."

I looked at Greg.

He nodded. "She's right."

"But aren't I supposed to call my lawyer?"

"Abby, you're not a suspect. She just wants to ask you a few questions. She's not going to shine a light in your eyes, or tie you to a rack."

"Then fire away," I said to prove I was both innocent and game.

"Is the dining room okay?"

"That would be fine," Investigator Sharp said in that high, girlish voice I found so annoying.

I led the way, limping. I was pretty sure my right ankle wasn't broken, but it was definitely sprained. I'd exchanged my hoops and stilts for sweats and slippers, but walking was still a chore.

"What happened to your foot?" At least the investigator could see the obvious.

"I fell."

"When?"

"It has nothing to do with the case, I assure you."

She let it drop and I showed her to the carver's chair at the head of my new dining room table. Actually, it isn't new at all, but seventeenth-century English. It is, however, new to me. At any rate, a normal person would have commented about how beautifully appointed the room was. Investigator Sharp seemed oblivious to taste. She reached into a snakeskin attaché case and removed a palm-sized tape recorder, which she set on the table in front of her. Then she crossed her long shapely legs, balancing a stenographer's pad on her knee.

I stared at the dinky device. "You're going to tape me?"

"Do you have a problem with that?"

"Well, no—but couldn't you just write everything down on your pad?"

"I suppose I could, but that would take too long. I plan to write down only those things which seem to be of obvious importance at the moment."

"But Greg said you only had a few questions!"

She tossed her blond locks in a dismissive manner. "Mrs. Timberlake, how well did you know the deceased?"

It was time to regain a little control. It was, after all, my house.

"First," I said, "please, call me Abby. I only kept Timberlake for professional reasons. The real Mrs. Timberlake is upstairs. Dead."

"I beg your pardon?"

"The *deceased*, as you call her. Her name is Tweetie Timberlake. She was married to my ex-husband. So you might say I knew her fairly well."

I'm not an expert at reading upside down, and her penmanship left a lot to be desired, but as far as I could tell, Investigator Sharp wrote everything down. Word for word. It took forever. Quite possibly she hadn't mastered some of the harder letters, like capital T's.

"Abby," she finally said, "you may call me Barb."

I nodded, but said nothing. Clearly she was trying to disarm me with this gesture of familiarity.

My silence didn't stop pen from moving on pad. "And how would you describe your relationship?"

"It was civil. Well, maybe not at first, but what can you expect? She snatched my husband out from under me—uh, I don't mean that literally—and disrupted my children's lives. But it's been several years, and I had made my peace with the woman. In fact, because of our age difference, it's almost like I saw her as another daughter."

"I see. So you completely got over your resentment?"

"Well, I suppose there were vestiges of—hey, I didn't use the word 'resentment,' did I?"

Barb smiled. "But would you say the word fits?"

"Not really. Sure, I remember what she did to my family, but I don't dwell on it. I certainly didn't wish her any harm. Like I said, I felt sort of motherly toward her. Lord knows the woman could have used a better one. You might even say Tweetie and I were friends—at the least we were united against a common enemy."

"Oh? Who?"

"Buford. My ex, and her present. They're still— well, *were*—still married. Tweetie was incapable of supporting herself, and since Buford is Charlotte's

finest divorce lawyer, alimony is not a given.
Tweetie had decided to stick it out until she was
sure of her options."

"I see. Tell me, why was the deceased incapable,
as you put it, of supporting herself?"

"Tweetie is the quintessential blond joke. Line
up ten of her and you get a wind tunnel. Give her
a, uh—" I suddenly remembered I was talking to a
blond. "Tweetie was a *bottle* blond," I added
hastily. "I'm sure that makes a difference."

Barb appeared unaffected by my reference to
color preference. "The second Mrs. Timberlake
never worked?"

I breathed a quiet sigh of relief. "She was working as an exotic dancer when Buford met her. But
she had no college or formal job training, and
would never have gone back to dancing. Not after
having a taste of the good life."

"I suppose a job as night clerk at a convenience
store was not an option?"

"Would it be for you? If you were in Tweetie's
circumstances, I mean? She may not have been accepted by everyone in her milieu, but she did a lot
of work for charity, and because of that, had a
good number of friends on the social register. No, I
think Tweetie's only option was to find another
mate with Buford's connections."

Barb's writing hand was a blur. "You certainly
seem to have done all right on your own."

I ran my fingers through hair the color of dark
chocolate. I'm genetically blest. Gray is only just
beginning to creep in along the temples, and it's

more silver than gray. Icing on the cake, Mama calls it.

"I had a passion for antiques," I said. "It's easier when you have a passion."

Barb vigorously underlined something. "Okay, let's talk about the party. Was Mrs. Timberlake an invited guest?"

"Of course. So was Buford. Only he had to be out of town on business."

"I see. Well, you certainly are a broad-minded woman, Abby."

I fell for the bait. "Look, I'd rather have invited Newt Gingrich and Dennis Rodman. I would have, too, if I'd thought they'd have come. The party was to impress people."

"I see. Were there crashers that you know of?"

"It was a costume party," I said irritably. "Some of the guests were able to completely disguise themselves."

Barb nodded. "Like the deceased."

"Oh, no! Tweetie didn't come as a knight. She came dressed as Little Bo Peep."

"Little Bo Peep?"

"She even brought a live sheep."

Barb scribbled furiously. "Who came as the knight?"

I shrugged. "I haven't the slightest. It never said a word."

"Who arrived at your party first? The knight, or Miss Peep?"

"Miss Peep, as I recall."

"Who was the first to leave?"

"Uh, well—that was a bit more confusing, seeing as how I had a virtual riot on my hands. Come to think of it, I can't remember either of them leaving. They certainly didn't throw potshots at me like some of the other guests."

Barb's pen hovered above the pad like it couldn't wait to deposit more ink. If indeed she was writing only the most important points, I could be in trouble.

"Abby, what do you mean when you say you had a virtual riot on your hands? What was going on?"

"Mama! That's what was going on. She came to the party dressed as Lady Godiva. If she'd come as Mary Poppins, I'm sure Lady Liberty wouldn't have dropped her torch. I tried to keep order, but they just wouldn't listen. What was I to do, but kick them all out?"

Apparently Barb found this amusing. She twittered like a schoolgirl who'd been told a naughty joke.

"You try having Mozella Wiggins as your mother!" I wailed. "She's more trouble than raising teenagers."

"I wouldn't know. I have no children."

"Well, take my word for it."

"I'll do that. Okay, Abby"— she scanned her notes—"do you recall any interaction between Miss Peep and the Tin Man during the party?" She smiled. "Before the riot?"

"No. In fact, it's like they both disappeared. I remember thinking how glad I was that Tweetie didn't sneak that stupid sheep into my house. She tried to bring it through the front door, you know."

"Ah, yes the sheep. I was just getting to that. Where is it now?"

"Heck if I know." I clapped my hands to my cheeks. "Oh my gosh, you don't think it's still tied up outside? If it's eaten my camellias I'll kill Tweetie—oops, that's not what I meant to say! It's just a figure of speech. I say that all the time. And not just me, either, everyone says that. I bet even you say that." I giggled nervously.

Barb's eyes made contact with mine, but I could no longer read their expression. "Who discovered the body?"

"Not me! It was Wynnell Crawford. I already told you that."

"Where were you at the time?"

"I was waiting for her at the top of stairs. We were going to go down together to check the windows and doors."

"What was she doing? Why were you waiting?"

"She was retrieving a machete I keep under the bed."

MACHETE she wrote in large block letters that I could read even though they were upside down. She underlined the word twice. Then she enclosed the C and turned it into a smiley face.

"It's safer than a gun," I explained quickly. "And it's really just an antique. I would never really use it, of course, unless someone broke into my house—" I clapped both hands over my mouth. Give me a thread and I would find some way to twist it into a hangman's noose.

Barb's pen did the flamenco and she was forced to turn the page to allow it more room. "How long was Mrs. Crawford out of your sight?"

"Just a minute or two. Trust me, she didn't have time to kill Tweetie and stuff her in that suit of armor. Besides, where would she have hidden the Bo Peep costume? And what about the person who came in the armor? Where did she disappear to?"

The tiny recorder had a tiny tape, and the machine shut itself off. Barb reversed the direction before answering. "That's a good question. But are you saying you think the perpetrator was female?"

"Huh?"

"You said *she*."

"I was being nonsexist. I never even saw the person inside the suit, so I don't know if *he* was male or female. It could have been either, you know."

"I see. Is this a genuine suit of armor?"

"Heavens no. It's a good copy though. I'll grant you that. But nobody I know would abandon a suit of genuine seventeenth-century Italian armor. Besides, a real suit of armor would weigh in the neighborhood of sixty pounds. It would be a real chore to lug that around just for a party."

"So you are saying that the person who wore it to your party had to be a male."

"Or a strong female," I said, and then immediately wished I hadn't.

She gave me the once over while I tried to look

as puny as possible. Apparently satisfied, she consulted her notes briefly.

"Abby, why didn't you kick out your friend, Mrs. Crawford, along with the rest of them?"

"Because she was drunk in bed."

The pen got a good workout. "Abby, what is your relationship to Mrs. Crawford?"

"Well, we're best friends. As close as gums and teeth. And we're colleagues. She owns the shop across the street."

"Have the two of you been getting along lately?"

"Of course. Sure, sometimes we have our—hey, you're not thinking I killed Tweetie, and that I'm trying to frame Wynnell, are you?"

"I haven't come to any conclusions," she said, without making eye contact. "I'm just gathering facts."

"Facts? I can't read most of what you're writing, but you're sure doing a lot of it. Frankly, Barbie—I mean Barb—I'd feel a lot better if I had my attorney present."

"Abby, you have not been arrested. There's really no need to involve him."

"It's a her."

"Well, you are free to cooperate or not. The decision is yours. But in all fairness, if you choose not to cooperate—well, let's just say there are certain implications to be considered."

I refuse to be bullied. Most of the time, perhaps due to my diminutive stature, folks want to protect me. But every now and then I run into someone who seems eager to push me around. When I was younger, I allowed the pushers to get me just to the edge of hysteria before I fought back. By now experience has taught me that it is less stressful, and far more effective, to resist the moment I feel I'm being compromised. If I'd only paid attention to my cat, I would have learned this far earlier in the game.

"This sounds like a threat," I said calmly.

"Threat?" Barb jabbed the off button on the miniature recorder. "Look here, Mrs. Timberlake, I'm just trying to do my job with as little interference as possible. You want your lawyer? Fine. But I'm warning you—"

I stood. The pain in my ankle was excruciating, but I'm pretty sure I didn't let it show.

"This interview is over."

Barb blinked. "As you wish."

"Terrific! Because I also wish you would leave my house."

"No can do. Not until I finish my job. First I need to speak to Mrs. Crawford."

8

Greg and Wynnell were in the kitchen sipping hot chocolate and eating cheese straws. On the stove a pot of fresh peanuts was boiling merrily. Under normal circumstances I would have plopped a deck of cards on the table and the three of us would have had a rousing game of Up and Down the Ladder. Alas, it was far from a normal evening. I had a throbbing ankle, and there were at least five people in my bedroom upstairs, one of whom was as dead as last Sunday's roast. Wynnell, to tell you the truth, didn't look a whole lot healthier.

She jumped when she saw me. "Abby!"

By contrast, Greg set his mug down casually. "How'd it go?"

"The woman is a witch," I said kindly. "She gets you to buddy up to her—insists you call her Barb—but the whole time she's waiting to pounce on you like a hen on a June bug."

Wynnell sipped noisily from her cup. "Were you cooperative, Abby?"

"Until she pushed me too far. Thank heavens I'd taken that Xanax."

Greg pulled me lightly into his lap. "Barb's new in the department. She has a different way of doing things."

Wynnell scowled. "Is she a Yankee? I didn't hear an accent."

"Barb's from California—*Southern* California—but she was born and raised in Raleigh. Anyway, she's pretty good at what she does."

"Says who?"

"Everyone, I guess. Sure, there was a little resistance when we first heard a woman was joining the department, but then we gradually warmed up to the idea."

"I bet y'all did. Some of y'all might even have overheated."

Greg chuckled. "Well, you can't deny she's a looker."

"Look, but don't touch." I slipped into a chair of my own.

"Hey, you're not jealous, are you?"

"Not on your life." I took a sip from his mug. "Wynnell, she wants to talk to you next."

Wynnell blanched, her black brows standing out like clumps of wet driftwood on a white sand beach. She was in the middle of swallowing, and apparently some of the liquid went down the wrong pipe.

"*Now?*" she gasped.

I leaned over and gave her a good hard slap on the back. "I'm afraid so."

"But I don't know anything. I was—well, I was, uh—"

"Passed out on my guest bed the entire evening?"

"Abby!" Greg said sternly. He gave Wynnell the thumbs-up sign. "Hey. You've got nothing to worry about, right?"

"Right."

"So just tell her the truth."

"Which she'll twist into a braid of a thousand strands," I mumbled.

"Abby!"

"But it's true! She took everything I said the wrong way."

"Abby, you're acting like a child."

"I am not!"

"But you are."

I turned to Wynnell. "Am I?"

"If the shoe fits," she said and took a loud slurp.

By then I'd had it with everyone. I stamped my size-four, realizing too late it was the wounded party. After a muffled scream and a few choice words, I got my act together.

"I'm out of here, guys. Will one of you please feed Dmitri before you lock up?"

Greg stood. He'd loom over me even if he were on his knees.

"But Abby, you just can't cut out like this. You may be needed for more questioning."

"Try me." I hobbled to the door and then re-membered that my pocketbook containing my keys was still upstairs. "Wynnell, may I borrow your car?"

"How will I get home?"

"Greg will take you, won't you, dear?"

He sighed. "Okay, but where will I find you?"

"You're the detective," I said. "Figure it out."

Every woman should have a sensitive male friend she can turn to when the going gets tough. I am fortunate in that I have two.

The Rob-Bobs live in a sumptuous townhouse they love to show off. Their guest room has an *authentic* Queen Anne bed. According to them it belonged to Anne herself. While I'm sure a queen slept in that bed, I doubt if it was Her Majesty. Still, the pair has a superb collection of first-rate antiques and the class with which to display them to their full advantage. The only trouble is, both men suffer from bad cases of revolving-door syndrome.

This is a chronic disease common among those in our trade. I've experienced severe bouts of this illness. One month I was deeply in love with a French fauteuil which I took home from my shop and placed lovingly beside my fireplace. The next month I replaced this heavily scrolled chair with a more blocky bergère that fit the location even better. It's not that I had fallen out of the love with the former, it's just that I had still to meet the latter. In other words, something better is always bound to come along, a point I have tried in vain to teach my children.

When you attend weekly auctions as I do, this

lesson is learned over and over again, but it is still a hard one to master. Since I own my own shop, I can draw from my inventory whenever I want. As a result my decor is constantly changing. Sometimes I envy Mama, who got locked in a time warp the day Daddy died, killed in a boating accident when a seagull with an enormous brain tumor dive-bombed us while we were waterskiing on Lake Wylie. Unlike her cronies, Mama never gets suckered into visiting furniture stores that promise no interest, and deferred payments until the cows come home. Mama never rearranges, never paints, and consequently never spends. Both her cash flow and contentment levels remain high.

Because the Rob-Bobs are even more fickle than I, visiting them is invariably a treat. But it is their warmth and understanding I enjoy most.

"Abby!" Rob Goldburg cried as he answered the door. He enclosed me in an embrace reeking of imported cologne commingled with party sweat. Still dressed as James Brolin, the man was undeniably handsome.

Bob Steuben, who originally hails from Toledo, is a little more reserved. He'd shed Babs's sequined gown in favor of chinos and a chambray shirt. Although he'd done a decent job of scrubbing off the makeup, traces of lip liner remained.

"Hey," he boomed in his trademark bass, "I was just stirring up a little nosh. You want a bite!"

Rob laughed. "I've been teaching Bob a little Yiddish. 'Nosh' seems to be his favorite word."

I glanced at the long case Bornholm clock in the

foyer. It was new to their digs, but appeared to be working. It was twelve minutes after midnight, a strange hour to be stirring up anything.

"Didn't Mama serve anything at her party?" I asked hopefully. Mama is an excellent cook capable of making ambrosia out of the most unlikely ingredients. She does not own a microwave, however, so instant treats are out of her arena.

"She didn't have time," Rob said. "You called and then the party just sort of fell apart. Actually, it never really began."

I felt wickedly exultant. I love my mama dearly, but she always has to steal the show—particularly if it's mine. She fainted during my wedding processional—somehow managed to land sprawled-eagle across the aisle—just I approached her pew. Daddy, who was used to Mama's shenanigans, whispered in my ear to just step over her. The congregation, taking their cue from us, ignored my prostrate progenitress, and she eventually hauled herself back into her seat. At least she was no longer lying there when I walked back down the aisle with Buford.

Bob nudged me. "So, Abby, you want to try my Down Under Surprise?"

"Well—"

"It's emu egg omelets," Rob warned me. "With kiwi fruit compote on the side."

I smiled. Bob is a serious gourmand. It didn't surprise me a bit that he was able to find emu eggs in Charlotte. At the moment, however, eggs of any size were unappealing.

"Maybe next time. Y'all mind if I crash here for the night?"

Both men beamed. "We already put mints on your pillow," Rob said. "Greg just called to let us know you were coming."

"He *did*?"

Bob led me to a settee done in rococo style with a ribband back. "You can park your tuchas here," he said. It wasn't a particularly comfortable place to rest my derriere, but since it had a genuine Thomas Chippendale provenance, who cared?

"What all did Greg have to say?"

"Primarily that he knew you were heading here, and that we should tuck you in."

"And kiss you good night," Rob said. Both men squirmed.

I laughed. "I can tuck myself in, thanks."

Rob pulled up a silk hassock. "He also mentioned that Tweetie's body was found stuffed in a suit of armor. Was it the same three-quarter Italian suit we saw at your party?"

I nodded.

Bob perched beside me on the settee. "Don't worry, Abby. It should be really easy for the police to trace a quality costume like that. There can't be that many rental shops in town."

Rob nodded. "Right. Although, it could be a privately owned costume. Abby, any theater people at your party?"

I must confess I wasn't really listening. "You know," I said, thinking aloud, "maybe it's not a costume at all, but a genuine suit of armor."

"What?" Both men were incredulous.

My cheeks burned with embarrassment. Although I carry quality merchandise in the Den of Antiquity, I'm not even in the same league with the Rob-Bobs. Their shop is on a par with any found in London, New York, or Paris. These men are experts.

"I just thought—well, it looked too real to be a costume. And it was heavy, too. Just lifting the visor took effort."

They couldn't help but exchange "poor Abby" looks.

"I was just thinking aloud," I wailed.

"Sweetie," Rob said, sitting on the other arm of the settee, "you're right. It might not be a costume at all. A lot of people ship these realistic copies of armor back from Europe."

"They do? Whatever for?"

"To put in their foyers," Bob boomed.

I could feel myself blush. "What a silly thing to do."

"It's some kind of an ego trip," Rob said. He patted my shoulder. "Invite anyone who's been to Europe recently?"

I choked back a gasp. "Buford and Tweetie. They did the grand tour this summer."

Rob's hand froze. "Abby, you're not suggesting that—"

"No!" I cried. "Buford would sleep with a porcupine, but he couldn't kill anyone."

Bob leaned forward, looking me gently in the eyes. "How can you be so sure?"

"Because he's the father of my children!"

Neither man spoke.

"Look, guys, Buford is a snake, I won't deny that. But he's slimy, not lethal."

"Uh-huh, Abby," they said in unison.

I stood. "Look, he didn't kill Tweetie, okay? And I'm going to prove it."

"How?" Rob asked softly.

"I'm going to find out who owns that suit, that's how."

"We'll do what we can to help," Bob said.

"Just tell us what to do," Rob agreed.

"Thanks." I thought for a moment. "I know you guys think I'm crazy, but just *suppose* this suit of armor isn't a costume and isn't a copy meant for some rich American's foyer. *Suppose* it's the real McCoy? Then the question becomes, who here in Charlotte is rich and savvy enough to own a suit of genuine seventeenth-century Italian armor?"

The men exchanged glances.

9

"Who?" I demanded. "Y'all know something, don't you? Is it one of y'all's clients?"

They sat stone-faced, mum as a pair of jade Buddhas.

"Come on!" I wailed. "Out with it!"

"You'll never believe it," Rob finally said.

My heart sank. "Oh no! But why? Y'all knew I was over my feelings of hate."

"Abby—"

"And when did you get the armor? Y'all never said anything about it?" To be perfectly honest, I was feeling more left out than horrified.

"Abby, we didn't do it. We didn't kill Tweetie."

"You *didn't*?"

The men burst into laughter. Rob's period of hilarity was mercifully short, but Bob switched from laughing to braying like a donkey. He can give C. J. a run for her money any day.

"Stop laughing at me! Rob, you just said I'd never believe it, so what was I to think?"

"Not that we killed Tweetie!"

I waved a hand impatiently. "Okay, I'm sorry. But then what is it I'd never believe?"

Bob brayed to a stop. "Who it is who collects genuine antique armor."

"*Who?*" We were beginning to sound like a bunch of owls.

"The Widow Saunders," Rob said smugly.

I looked at him in astonishment. Mrs. Gavin Lloyd Saunders is one of Charlotte's most reclusive millionaires. If it wasn't for the plaques around town denoting her many civic contributions, and the occasional photo on the *Observer*'s society page, I wouldn't have believed she existed. I have never met her, nor do I personally know anyone who has. But then again, there are many layers to Charlotte society, as I'm sure there are everywhere. The higher one climbs, the more one discovers there are new heights to scale. For a middle-class peon like myself, the pinnacle will remain forever shrouded in the mists of protocol.

"How do you know this?" I demanded.

The men grinned. "Because," Rob said, "we've been to her house."

"Get out of town!"

Rob shook his handsome head.

I grabbed a bony chunk of Bob's shoulder. "He's kidding, right?"

"He's not kidding. She had us over to the house for an appraisal last week."

"What was it? What did you appraise?" Considering the widow's reputation, I wouldn't have been surprised to learn it was the Holy Grail the Rob-Bobs had been asked to tag.

"Sorry, Abby, but we're not allowed to tell."

"*What?*"

"She asked we keep it confidential."

"But we're friends. We break confidences all the time. Just last week you told me that Linda Gettlefinger had her eyes done, and she made you promise not to tell."

They looked sheepish, but declined to comment. "*Please!*"

Rob spread his long patrician fingers in a gesture of finality. "Give it up, Abby. But we can tell you that the Widow Saunders has the finest private collection of armature either of us has ever seen."

"Not that we spent much time looking at it," Bob said with a nasty wink. "There were other things to occupy our attention."

"Bob!" Rob said sharply.

I gave it up as Rob suggested. There was no point in trying to wrench that secret out of them.

"Would y'all be willing to introduce me to the Widow Saunders?"

"But Abby—"

"I'd like to study a real suit of seventeenth-century armor," I said quickly. "Just to satisfy myself that the armor Tweetie was found in wasn't real."

They nodded reluctantly.

"All right," Rob said, "we'll do what we can. But it may take a few days to come up with a good excuse. She's a suspicious old thing. I forgot to tell her Bob was coming with me and she nearly freaked out. Thought he worked for the IRS."

"Tell her I'm a history buff."

"That might do the trick. Like I said, I'll think about it."

"In the meantime," Bob said, "there are fresh sheets on the Queen Anne, and breakfast will be brought to you at eight."

He was true to his word. At precisely eight in the morning I was awakened by a gentle touch on my shoulder. I sat up to find a lap table astride my hips. Atop the table was a silver tray set with hand-painted Limoges china. A neatly folded white linen napkin sported a complement of sterling cutlery in the Sir Christopher pattern.

I studied the dishes. A pot of hot chocolate. A toasted bagel with lox and cream cheese. A rasher of bacon. A small plate of fresh sliced honeydew melon. And three tiny poached eggs.

My sigh of relief cooled the eggs and chilled the melon further. "No more emu eggs?" I said jokingly.

Bob blinked. "Oh, we still have plenty of those, but as everyone knows, emu eggs are for brunches and late-night suppers."

"Of course. I knew that."

"These are guinea eggs."

I smiled. An egg was an egg, wasn't it? Just as long as it came from a bird smaller than I.

"They look delicious," I said sincerely. "Thanks."

Bob sat on the edge of the bed. "You need a good breakfast. Especially after what you went through last night."

"Last night?"

"Tweetie," he said simply.

"Oh my God! I can't believe I didn't remember!"

"It's normal to block things out, Abby."

"But I remembered the eggs—"

"Knock, knock." Rob stood in the doorway holding a cordless phone. He nodded at me. "It's for you. Buford."

The chill that ran up my spine was enough to give Santa shivers. I started shaking all over.

"What will I say?" I whispered desperately.

One of Bob's warm hands found mine. "Just tell him what you know. He can't blame you, Abby."

Rob handed me the phone. "You want us to stay?"

For some reason their kindness made me feel like a big baby. "No, I can handle this," I said resolutely and took the phone. I waited until they'd tiptoed out of the room before speaking into the phone. "Hello?"

"Abby?"

"Yes, Buford."

"Are you all right?"

I held the phone away from my ear and stared at it. Everything seemed normal to me.

"Buford, is that really you?"

"Of course it is. Who else would it be? Abby, Greg called me with the terrible news and—"

"I'm really sorry, Buford. You have my deepest

sympathy. I know you think I didn't like Tweetie—hated her even—but it isn't true. Why, we had lunch together just last week to discuss—"

"Hey, Abby, I believe you."

"You *do*?"

"Yeah, I do."

"Then why are you calling?"

"Because Greg said you were really upset. Look, Abby, I really am in Tokyo this time. Just listen." Presumably he held the machine away from his ear because I heard the din of voices, some of which may have been Japanese. "You hear that?"

"Yes," I said warily.

"I'm at the train station. I'm on a flight that leaves from Narita Airport in two hours. It's the last direct flight to the States tonight, so I have to make this connection. I would have booked an earlier one, but everything was full. Anyway, I just needed to hear how you are, and to tell you that I'll be there as soon as humanly possible."

"Thanks." I didn't know what else to say.

"Oh, and Abby, I've called Malcolm and told him to get in touch with you. Whatever you need, you just tell him."

With that Buford hung up. I stared at the phone in my hands until the poached guinea eggs on my plate were as cold as hail pellets. I was still staring when Rob rapped softly on the door frame.

"You have a visitor," he said.

"Who?"

"A gentleman by the name of Malcolm Biddle. Abby, isn't that Buford's junior law partner?"

"His partner from hell," I corrected him. "Mr. Satan himself. Where is he?"

"In the living room. Shall I show him in?"

"Not on your life. I'll meet him out there."

10

You can't get any lower, if you ask me, than to ditch your wife while she's in the hospital having a hysterectomy. But that's just what Malcolm did. He dumped Jenny in favor of a tart named Miranda. And to think this man had the nerve to expect an invitation to my party!

For any doubters of karma out there, Miranda left Malcolm just three weeks later. The new object of the bimbo's affection was a Carolina Panther. But apparently the burly ballplayer had chimes Miranda couldn't ring, because shortly after their tryst began, he was caught soliciting male fans at the state welcome station in Pineville.

At any rate, I detest Malcolm. I did my best to make that clear to him. I choked down Bob's breakfast—which might have actually tasted pretty good under other circumstances—took a long hot bath, and dressed slowly. Only when I felt totally in control did I deign to hobble into Beelzebub's presence.

He looked up from one of the Rob-Bob's antique magazines. An objective person might find Malcolm attractive. He has regular features and a solid build. His hair is his own, and while I can't vouch for the provenance of his teeth, he seems to have a full contingent. Yet, while his complexion isn't particularly oily, he seems to exude an air of slipperiness.

"Hey, you all right?" he asked and arranged his lips in a smirk.

"Hey, yourself. You know, Malcolm, I really don't need you checking up on me."

He closed the magazine and tossed it onto the silk hassock. "Buford's orders."

"You're his junior law partner, for crying out loud. You're not his errand boy."

"That's easy for you to say. You're divorced. He still signs my checks." He laughed. "Come to think of it, I guess he still signs yours, too."

"Not hardly. If you pulled your weight in the firm you'd know better. Buford played his good old boy card and got out of paying alimony altogether."

Malcolm whistled. "Man, that had to hurt. But if you hook up with me, Abby, I won't treat you that way."

"What?" I couldn't believe my ears.

"What do you say, Abby? Just one date."

"Not for all the bran in St. Petersburg," I growled. "You're supposed to be comforting me, not hitting on me."

"Why can't it be both?"

"Out!" I pointed to the door.

"Calm down," he had the nerve to say.

"Don't tell me what to do!" I hobbled forward threateningly. "I said 'out'!"

"Who's going to make me?"

"Me. And if I need to, I'll get help."

"You mean *them*?"

The Rob-Bobs had discreetly disappeared into what they so charmingly call "the salon." The muted strains of classical music could be heard through the closed door.

"Either one of them could wipe the floor with you," I said through clenched teeth.

He had the temerity to laugh.

I shook a finger at him in warning. "Rob has a black belt and Bob a brown."

"You're kidding."

"I'm not." And I wasn't. Rob did indeed have a black belt. It went nicely with his best suit. As for Bob's brown belt, I bought the matching corduroys myself.

Malcolm slid out of the rococo settee. Mercifully, there were no grease stains left behind.

"Okay, I'm outta here. But if Buford asks, I did my duty, right?"

"If you say so."

"Too bad about Tweetie," he said, in the same tone he might have used to refer to milk gone sour.

"Tweetie was no saint," I said tightly, "but she didn't deserve to die."

"Yeah, well, we all have to go sometime."

"You got that right." I gave him a not-so-gentle shove toward the door.

Caught off guard, Malcolm staggered a few steps. But when he regained his balance, he spread his legs in a stance of defiance.

"We have to talk," he said.

I wasted no time. "Rob! Bob!"

My buddies must have been sitting with their heads next to the speakers. No help was forthcoming.

"We have to talk," Malcolm said again.

I glared at closed salon doors. "We have nothing to talk about, Mr. Biddle."

"I think we do. I think there's been a big misunderstanding."

"On your part maybe," I snapped.

"Yeah, I guess so."

"What?"

"You're right, Abby. I got it all wrong."

"You can say that again."

To my astonishment—and disbelief, I might add—Malcolm underwent a metamorphosis right in front of my eyes. The slime just seemed to melt away, uncovering a man who looked as vulnerable as my Charlie did his first day of school.

"I'm sorry, Abby," he said. There was not a trace of sarcasm in his voice. "I was given the wrong impression and never bothered to check things out for myself."

"What things?" I hissed. The man better not be playing me for a fool.

"Buford—well, let's just say I was led to believe that you had the hots for me."

"What?" If my shriek didn't bring the Rob-Bobs running, nothing would.

The doors to the salon stayed tightly closed as Malcolm continued. "It's all my misunderstanding, of course, but I thought you were just playing hard to get."

"That's the most ridiculous thing I ever heard!"

"Yeah, I realize that now. Again, I'm really sorry."

I took a deep breath. "Look, even if that were true, this would be a hell of a time to hit on me. Finding a dead woman under your bed is traumatizing."

"Yeah, you're right. That was really stupid of me. There is no excuse for my behavior."

I stared at Malcolm. He hardly looked like the same man. Was it possible I had been at least partly wrong about him?

"What you did to your wife was despicable," I said. "Do you have an excuse for that?"

He shook his head remorsefully. "I shouldn't have left her at a time like that. Sure, she was having an affair with her doctor—"

"Come off it! *You* were having an affair with a bimbo named Miranda."

He blinked. "Say what?"

"Give it up, Malcolm. Everybody knows. The fact that you got dumped is only half of what you deserved."

As if wounded by my words, he clutched his middle dramatically. "I need to sit."

"I said give it up. Your heart, if you ever had one, would be higher than that."

He pushed past me and virtually threw himself down on the settee. "It's not my heart," he gasped. "It's an ulcer."

"Right."

"You don't have to believe me." He took a couple of deep breaths, his handsome face twisted in a grimace. "What you said before—I never touched Miranda."

"Sure you did. Tweetie told me."

He smiled crookedly. "Ah, Tweetie. She would have said that. Miranda was her best friend. The doctor was Miranda's husband. Apparently Tweetie twisted things around a bit."

"Is that right? Well, I'll just ask her!" Realizing what I'd said, I clapped a hand over my mouth. I clapped it hard.

"Well, you can't do that now, can you?" he said softly.

I plopped my mouthy self on the hassock. Tweetie had told me the tragic details of Malcolm's affair over lunch at the Red Lobster. I remember that day clearly; the restaurant had inexplicably run out of shrimp scampi and I'd had to console myself with an extra cheese biscuit. At any rate, my ex-husband's current wife had made me promise not to tell a soul, and so far I'd kept my word. They only people I'd shared the sad story with were Mama, Wynnell, C. J., and my daughter, Susan. Oh, and the Rob-Bobs, but that goes without saying. Surely Tweetie hadn't meant that I not tell *them*.

"You really didn't cheat on your wife while she was in the hospital for a hysterectomy?"

He looked stunned. "A hysterectomy? Is that what Tweet said?"

"Yes. You could have at least waited until she was home again."

"It was liposuction, and she didn't even stay overnight."

"Oh my."

He shook his head. "That Tweetie. She really had it in for me, didn't she?"

"Why was that?" I asked weakly.

"Because I convinced Buford not to run for the Senate. Apparently she had big dreams. Senator's wife, then governor's wife, and then finally First Lady."

The thought of Tweetie Bird in the White House made me shudder. I don't mean to be disrespectful of the dead, but if that had happened, during the very next election America would have voted into office a communist government. Either that, or a fundamentalist right-wing government so strict they required their head of state to take a vow of celibacy.

"I'm so sorry, Malcolm. I got the story all wrong." I didn't know what else to say.

Although Malcolm smiled, I could see he was still in pain. "That's all right. Now that everything's straight, between us, let me ask you again. Are *you* all right, Abby?"

I told Malcolm that I was not all right. How does one erase such a gruesome sight from one's memory? How does one go to sleep in a house where a woman was brutally murdered? Now I'm not saying I believe in ghosts, and I'm not saying I do—well, okay, I do.

It seems perfectly logical to me that a soul which has been forced from the body under sudden and unusual circumstances might be confused, unable to find its way to the spirit realm. Or in some cases, unwilling. I was touring the Civil War battlefield of Manassas—where the Battle of Bull Run was fought—one foggy morning when I got separated from my group. As I was stumbling about the moors, barely able to see my feet, I encountered a beautiful young woman in period costume. Thinking that she was a guide, I asked her for directions back to the exhibit hall. After all, the dewy grass was soaking my shoes and I had to use the restroom—desperately—or even more of me was going to get wet. There is no shame in cutting one's losses, you know.

The auburn-haired beauty had a wicker picnic hamper hanging on one arm, a coarse brown blanket tucked under the other. Her large gray eyes appeared to see right through me.

"Which way to the front?" she asked.

"I beg your pardon?"

"My Edward is serving under Brigadier General Irvin McDowell. I have come to watch righteousness prevail."

"Oh, a Yankee," I sniffed on Wynnell's behalf.

Instead of responding, the young woman simply disappeared. Just like that, she evaporated before my eyes, melding with the fog. As she did so, I felt the hair on my arms stand up.

Later, back at the information center, I learned that the women of Washington had come out in mass, laden with picnic baskets, to monitor the battle's progress from distant hills. Much later, in a poem, the title of which I now forget, I read of a maiden named Emily "with eyes so fair" who, while on her way to watch her lover triumph at Bull Run, wandered afield and was killed by a stray cannonball. According to the poem, the missile was launched by the Federals, quite possibly by her sweetheart himself.

At any rate, even if you do not believe in ghosts, surely you will agree that the joy I once experienced living in my new house was now a thing of the past. Tweetie herself might not return to haunt me, but the memory of her corpse would. No, there was nothing left for me to do but sell the house. Undoubtedly news of the murder was in the morning *Observer* and on television, and only a ghoul would make me an offer.

Malcolm gave me hope, however, because before he left he gave me the name of a contractor who could remodel the master bedroom in such a way that I wouldn't recognize it, yet the integrity of the house would remain unchanged. Apparently this fellow made a living redoing rooms in which folks have died, and murders were his specialty. I thanked Malcolm, apologized again, and was in the process of closing the front door behind him when I heard the voices in the stairwell. So loud were they that even the Rob-Bobs, sequestered behind their salon door, heard them—or so they told me later.

"Abby's not going to forgive us just because you promise to give her a ride," the first one said.

"What if I promise not to buck?"

I sighed in resignation. There was no point in trying to avoid Mama and C. J. It would be like a child trying to outrun puberty. Unless you were Michael Jackson, you didn't stand a chance.

"Abby's always been afraid of horses," Mama said. It wasn't true, of course. "Maybe that's where we went wrong last night."

"My Granny Ledbetter always wanted to own a horse," C. J. said, launching into one of her infamous Shelby stories. "Only she and my granddaddy were too poor to buy one. Then one day, for Granny's birthday, Granddaddy dressed up the milk cow, Clarabelle, to look like a horse. He tied a fake mane around the cow's neck and glued some extra hair to her tail.

"Man, did Granny ever love her horse. She rode Clarabelle—only she was called Trigger now— around the farm so many times that the poor thing up and died. Of course Granny was very upset, but she was a practical woman, and like I said, she was very poor. Anyway, she had Granddaddy butcher Trigger, and that night they sat down to the best meal they'd had in years.

"Well, Granny couldn't get over how good the

horsemeat tasted. This was right after the war, and folks in France had even less to eat than we did here. So Granny canned what was left of Trigger and sent it to our French cousins in Paris. Back then no one in France had ever tasted horsemeat, you see. But they all thought they had when they tasted Trigger, and, well, the rest is history. To this very day horsemeat is very popular in France, and all because Granny wanted a horse."

"I don't think Ledbetter is a French name," Mama said skeptically.

The women emerged from the stairwell onto the landing and I breathed a huge sigh of relief. Mama was back in her uniform of Donna Reed–era duds. The vintage ensemble consisted of pink and white gingham dress with full circle skirt held aloft by layers of crinolines, pink hat and gloves, pink shoes, and her ubiquitous pearls. The last was a gift from my daddy, and to my knowledge Mama has never taken them off. Not even to shower.

"Mama," I said, just as calmly as if I'd been expecting her, "aren't you pushing it with the pink? I mean, isn't that a spring color? Why, today's the first day of November." I know that was cruel of me, but people who take fashion so seriously, albeit four decades late, deserve to have their noses tweaked. Besides, Mama made me wear an off-white wedding gown, on account of walking down the aisle in snow-white would have been a lie.

Mama, who wouldn't be caught dead wearing white between Memorial Day and Labor Day, turned the color of her pumps. She patted her pearls, a sure sign of distress.

"I'm planning ahead. Our Saviour," she said referring to her church, "is putting together a new directory for spring, so I'm having my picture taken today. How would it look if folks see me wearing fall colors next April, when the booklet comes out?"

"Well—"

"Besides, Abby, I didn't come all the way up here to talk about fashion. I came to give you this."

She handed me a *black* envelope.

11

I stared at the strange packet. It appeared to be made out of black construction paper, folded and taped to resemble a business envelope in size and shape. A small rectangle of white paper had been glued to the front side, and upon it my name stood out in bold red letters.

"This was under the door, Abby. I thought you might want to have it."

"Oh Abby, you look worried," C. J. said. She turned to Mama. "I told you we should have opened it first."

Mama thrust the letter at me. "I don't think it's a bomb, dear. I tried holding it up to the light but—"

"Mama! You *did* open it first, didn't you!"

She hung her head, which made her just my height. "I was just looking out for you, dear."

"For shame," I said.

"For shame," C. J. agreed.

I snatched the strange black envelope from Mama and ripped it open. In the process, I ripped its content, a single sheet of typing paper. Not that it mattered. The message was written on only one half. Red block letters, drawn with a felt-tip pen, spelled out three simple words. *You will pay*.

Dazed, I let envelope and papers flutter to the floor. I've already paid enough to last a lifetime. I paid when Daddy died. Mama didn't mean to take her grief out on me, but I was handy, and older than my brother, Toy. I paid when Buford and I got divorced. Never mind that he got custody of Charlie. In the kids' eyes, I was to blame for the fact that their father took up with a woman young enough to be their sister.

C. J. picked up my trash. "Oh, Abby, you don't think it's Buford, do you?"

"Buford?" Mama snapped. "Why Buford?"

C. J. shrugged. "Maybe because he thinks Abby is somehow responsible for Tweetie's murder. It happened at her house, didn't it?"

Mama gave C. J. a warning glare. "It *wasn't* Buford. He's a snake all right, but he's also the father of my two precious grandchildren. Buford would never hurt their mother. No, it's probably just one of those people who was bad-mouthing Abby at my house last night."

I snapped out of my reverie. "Who was bad-mouthing me?"

"Why, everyone, dear."

"Names," I hissed. "I want names."

"Well, there was Moses—I mean, Alan Bills. Said he'd never driven so far for nothing before. Said he had a better time the night he rented *Ishtar*."

C. J. nodded. "I loved that movie. But I don't

think it was Mr. Bills who sent you this note. I think it was either Geppetto or Pinocchio."

Mama scowled. She hates to be challenged.

"Why is that?"

"Because I heard them say they were so mad at Abby, they were never going to shop at the Den of Antiquity again."

"Not them, too!" I wailed.

Mama sniffed. "They may have been mad at Abby, but they weren't half as mad as Neptune and the mermaid. They said they'd had to give up a party at the mayor's."

C. J.'s eyes widened. "The mayor? Wow! Wait until Granny Ledbetter hears that I know someone who knows the mayor."

"Lynne Meredith was lucky to have even been invited to my party," I mumbled. "The mayor indeed!"

"What did you say?" Mama asked.

"I said that when she gets to heaven, Lynne Meredith will ask to see the upstairs."

C. J. giggled. "Ooh, Abby, you're bad."

"You're darn tooting. What else did my ungrateful guests have to say?"

"Does Irene count?" Mama asked. "I mean, she's your shop assistant, and she had to come."

"Is *that* what she said?"

They nodded.

"Well, spare me the details."

"You sure?" Mama asked. "Because I'd want to know if it was me."

"Is it about my party, or work?"

"Both. But mostly work."

I sighed and ushered them inside the Rob-Bobs' apartment. Their neighbors didn't need to know what a Scrooge I was—well, in Irene's eyes at any rate. I don't care what anyone says, I am not obligated to pay for my employee's Lasik surgery. Not at a thousand dollars an orb. Irene should pay for the procedure herself, or else content herself with the bifocals, for which my plan does provide.

"Spill it," I said, closing the door behind me.

"Well, dear, Irene said it was no surprise Tweetie was found dead under your bed. Not after that fight you two got into last week."

I clutched my chest and staggered backward until my thighs found the silk hassock. Only then did I allowed my knees to give out.

"Irene thinks I killed Tweetie?" I asked weakly.

Mama pranced over to pat my shoulder. "There, there, dear. She said you had a good reason."

"Yeah," C. J. agreed heartily. "She said Tweetie told you she showed Charlie some porn pictures. Of *her*, right?"

Was that it? Irene Cheng was going to have to do a better job of eavesdropping. What Tweetie said to me was that Charlie was surfing the Net and came upon some old pictures of Tweetie, taken in her pre-Buford days. My son had confronted his stepmother, who confessed immediately, and then came straight to me to clear up the matter. My response was a brief lecture about the far-reaching consequences of one's behavior. While my tone might have conveyed my annoyance—no young man should have to see his stepmother topless, even if the underlying structure is manmade—by no means did we have a fight.

"Irene needs to spend more time with our customers, and less time exercising her ears. Tweetie and I did not fight."

Mama clucked dismissively. "No one's blaming you, Abby. Well—except maybe for Irene. I'm not. I know if I were you, I certainly would have had a few harsh words to say. My poor grandson—"

The Rob-Bobs' phone rang, and was picked up in the salon after the second ring. A few seconds later the doors finally opened.

"Oh," Rob said, his voice registering surprise at the sight of Mama and C. J. He couldn't possibly have heard the women. "Uh, Abby, it's for you."

"Me?" I rolled my eyes desperately to indicate I'd like privacy.

Rob winked. "In here would be fine."

In a strange way I felt grateful to Tweetie for dying. In the four years I've known the Rob-Bobs, I'd been inside the salon only once before. And that first time it was still an empty room. I couldn't wait to see the treasures of their inner sanctum.

I stared at the room in disbelief. Could it be possible I was hallucinating? Maybe a flashback to something ingested during my college days? Like President Clinton, I, too, had been unable to inhale. But brownies, now that was another story. Perhaps one of the so-called Alice B. Toklas brownies I'd scarfed down had contained something more powerful than marijuana.

The Rob-Bobs' Holy of Holies was a holy nightmare of decorating. The room, which had terrific possibilities, due to its ceiling height and a plentitude of floor-to-ceiling windows, was almost unrecognizable. The walls had been papered with a faux leather finish, and the windows shrouded with heavy brown velvet drapes. The main piece of furniture was a double La-Z-Boy recliner with a pine console connecting the two chairs. The upholstery was burgundy, a color not repeated elsewhere in the room's spare furnishings. The focus of the room was a large screen television that had its own black plastic cabinet.

Even more appalling than the decor was the fact that Bob was sitting in one of the two recliners watching *The Rugrats*. He turned to see me enter, and then turned away, blushing. From then on, although the television was on mute, Bob seemed intently interested in the cartoon kiddies' escapades. That was fine with me. I was going to have a hard time looking either of the men in the face again.

I picked up the receiver, which was lying on the console next to a bowl of Frosted Flakes. "Hello?"

"Mrs. Timberlake, this is Captain Keffert. Please don't hang up."

I feigned surprise. "Why would I hang up? That would be rude."

"Then you're not sore?"

"About?" Experience has taught me never to close the door on a customer. They don't have to like you to buy something—although it helps. The reverse is certainly true. A fool's money is just as valuable as a friend's, and as the adage says, is soon parted.

"Heck, I'll come right out and say it. I was a bit rough with you last night, and I apologize."

"Apology accepted," I said brightly. "Does that mean you're not going to return the Queen Anne period secretary?"

"Absolutely. You don't think I'd let a little oversight like not being invited to your party get in the way of our doing business together, do you?"

I counted to ten, taking a deep breath with every digit. "Whatever, dear."

"Yes, well, I'm glad we got that squared away."

"So, to what do I owe the honor of this call?" Having raised two teenagers, I have fine-tuned the subtleties of sarcasm.

"Mrs. Timberlake—uh, do you mind if I call you Abby?"

"May I call you Richard?"

"Captain would be fine," he said archly. "Mrs. Timberlake, I was watching the news this morning and—"

"Oh, no! Was it on?" Of course it was. It had to have been. Yet the Rob-Bobs, darn their considerate hides, hadn't said a thing.

"They didn't have many details, Mrs. Timberlake. They just said that the other Mrs. Timberlake had been found dead in a suit of armor. I was—"

"Did they mention it happened at my house?"

"Yes, of course. That's how I knew to contact

you. When I got your machine, I called the shop. Your assistant, Mrs. Cheng, I believe, suggested I call here."

"What's she doing in on a Sunday?" I wailed. "We're closed!"

"Yes, well, I thought you would be. But I took a chance anyway." He cleared his throat in an officious way. "Mrs. Timberlake, about that cuirass I saw on TV—"

I stifled a gasp. "Say what?"

"Mrs. Timberlake, a cuirass is a three-quarter suit of armor made for a cavalryman. A cuirassier. But then again, you already know that."

I jiggled a pinky tip in my free ear to make sure it was hearing right. "Captain, are you some sort of armor expert?"

His laugh was a short bark, like that of a Doberman to which someone has thrown a steak. "Well, I wouldn't say that. But I do know a few things."

"I see. And they were showing my—well, this cuirass on TV?"

"Only for a few seconds, but I thought I recognized the closed burgonet. It's seventeenth-century Italian, right?"

"How do you know—I mean, is it?"

"Mrs. Timberlake, I was hoping you'd tell me."

"Uh, I think it's from that period."

"Mrs. Timberlake, let me get right down to brass tacks. How much are you asking?"

"I beg your pardon?"

"For the damn suit of armor," he growled. "Thirty thousand? Forty?"

"It isn't for sale," I huffed.

"Well, I won't pay you a nickel over fifty. Not without some special provenance attached. Is there one?" He sounded hopeful.

"How should I know?" I practically shouted. "I never saw that armor before last night!"

"Okay, play hard to get. I suppose this is part of your fun. But one hundred thousand even is my last offer. And for that I expect authentication from at least two other sources. And those funny boys you call friends don't count."

My shrieks made Bob jump. Rob, who'd been standing beside me the whole time, backed away as if he'd seen a living corpse.

"Captain Keffert! The armor is not mine! I don't know who it belongs to, and even if I did, it wouldn't do you any good. There's a body in it, for pity's sake!"

The Doberman, finished with his meal, had a good long laugh. "It's police evidence. I understand. All I want is first dibs on it. Isn't that what you young people say?"

"We young people slam down the phone when we're totally pissed off," I said with surprising calmness. But slam the phone I did.

12

The Rob-Bobs, bless their hearts, were exceedingly understanding when I told them I didn't have the energy to deal with Mama and C. J. further. They reluctantly gave me the Widow Saunders's address, then they parted the heavy brown drapes, pried a window open, and watched protectively while I negotiated the fire escape. Later, they told me they made the women wait another half-hour before telling them I was gone.

You can bet the first thing I did was drive out over to my shop, the Den of Antiquity. It's located on Selwyn Aveune, just five shady blocks from the Rob-Bobs' condominium, and I could have walked. At any rate, I parked Wynnell's car in front of her shop and dashed across the street to mine. Irene hadn't even locked the door, and although there is a string of alpine cowbells hanging on it, I managed to reach behind and hold it in place while I sneaked in. I was upon my employee before she knew what hit her.

"What are you doing here?" I demanded.

Irene, who was seated behind my desk, a large book spread open before her, jumped. It would be an exaggeration to say her head hit the ceiling, but her knees really did clatter the middle desk drawer.

"Oh God, Abby, you scared the crap out of me!"

"I *said*, what are you doing here?"

Irene patted her chest and took a few dramatic breaths. "I'm improving myself."

I grabbed the book and tilted it. The jacket had been removed from the heavy tome, but the gold lettering was still faintly visible on the green cloth cover. *Becoming a Successful Antique Dealer: Everything You Kneed to Know About the Business in Ten Easy Lessons.* The author was Eric von Dentheart, someone I'd never heard of.

"What's this?"

"A book."

"I can see that. But why are you reading it here? And on a Sunday?"

"I'm teaching myself the trade."

"Is that so? Well, you're not going to get that much from a book."

"I think I am. This is a very thorough, well-organized book. It has practical lessons, but you need to be in a real shop to do them."

"So you come here after hours?"

"But, Abby, I didn't think you'd mind. Lesson five is about how to sell slow-moving inventory. Remember that pile of antique Amish quilts you had sitting on that walnut table by the door? Well,

I sold all five of them this morning to the first lady who walked in."

I whirled. Not only were the quilts gone, but so was the table. In fact, my shop looked entirely different. It was much emptier, and nothing was in its assigned place.

"What's going on?" I demanded. "Where is everything?"

Irene tapped the book smugly. "Sold a lot of it yesterday while you were home getting ready for the so-called party. But some of the stuff I just moved around to display it better. No offense, Abby, but you don't have the best taste."

"I beg your pardon?"

"Well, just look at you."

I looked, but could see nothing wrong. I was still wearing the sweats I'd put on before the police arrived, but they weren't dirty or anything. On the other hand, Irene, when she's not dressed like the Statue of Liberty, always wears skirts. Sometimes the skirts have matching tailored jackets, sometimes color-coordinated sweaters. But she is, I'll admit, always neat as a pin.

"There was a body found under my bed," I reminded her. "I don't always dress this way."

"Oh, it isn't just your clothes, Abby. Why, take your house—"

"Leave my decorating style out of this," I snapped. "Irene, how long have you been operating after hours?"

"Well, just yesterday and this morning. And

Tuesday night after you went home. Abby, there's no sense in turning away eager customers."

"I don't see anybody beating the door down now."

"That's because a lot of them are still in church. But the eight o'clock service is almost over at the Church of the Holy Comforter. Business will be booming in a few minutes."

"No, it won't," I said with perverse satisfaction. "Nobody knows we're open."

Irene gave me a triumphant smile. Either that or she was fighting a bad case of gas.

"Yes, they do. I put an ad in this morning's *Observer*."

"You *what*?"

"Don't get your knickers in a knot, Abby. I paid for it with my own money."

I made her vacate *my* chair, and sat heavily. "Why?"

Irene waved her well-clothed arms. "Someday this shop is going to be mine. When that day comes I want a large and savvy clientele. Those ladies at Holy Comforter know their stuff. They buy more than just quilts."

To squelch the beginnings of a headache, I dug into my temples with ten fingers. "What makes you so damn sure I'm going to sell this place. And why to you?"

"Don't be such a goofball, Abby. You know you weren't cut out to be a businesswoman. Anyway, as soon as you marry Greg you're going to want to settle down and be the perfect little wife—no reference to your size intended. When you put the shop up for sale, I plan to buy it."

"Oh, do you?"

She nodded vigorously, her long black hair rising and falling like the flapping of raven wings. I haven't seen that much self-confidence since Muhammad Ali's interview with Mike Douglas almost forty years ago.

"While you're making plans," I said cleverly, "would you like to buy my house?"

Irene snorted. "Now you are being ridiculous. Who in their right minds would want a house where someone was murdered? Nobody, that's who!"

That irritated me to no end, especially since I felt the same way. To punish her for her observation, I resorted to an old trick. One I learned from my children. It's called Change the Subject.

"What business did you have telling Captain Keffert I was spending the night with the Rob-Bobs?"

Her eyes widened slightly. "He asked where you were. What was I supposed to do? Lie?"

"But how did you know my whereabouts?"

Irene is twenty-nine, but she arranged her features in a smirk worthy of any teenager. "I have my ways."

I was tempted to fire her on the spot. But what would my grounds be? I couldn't fire her for laziness. Or incompetence. Surely opening the shop without my permission was an offense worthy of a dismissal, but did I really want to live with the consequences? I was debating the ramifications of just such a move when the door opened with the clanging of bells and in trooped a bevy of eager females in Episcopal-length hemlines. Eight o'clock mass at the Church of the Holy Comforter was apparently over.

I promised the Rob-Bobs not to disclose the location of Widow Saunders' mansion, and I am a woman of my word. But if you continue on Selwyn Avenue north, turn right on Sherwood, then left on Hampton, you'll undoubtedly find it. If I gave you the house number, I wouldn't need to tell you that it was the enormous Georgian brick structure surrounded by a brick and wrought-iron fence, and that the driveway was guarded by a pair of snarling marble lions, perched atop pillars so large they might be gatehouses. A similar, but smaller, pair of brick posts guards the entrance to the walk. These support a wrought-iron gate in the shape of a lyre, and are topped by grimacing griffins. You really can't miss them.

Wynnell's '99 Grand Am is in good condition, but not in keeping with the manor. In order not to arouse undue suspicion, I parked in front of a more modest home a block and a half farther up the street. I always wanted to be an actress—my brother, Toy, claims he's an actor out in California— so acting casual under the circumstances was well within my capabilities. I strolled up the sidewalk and when I reached the pair of smaller pillars, I turned and nonchalantly tried the gate. Thank heavens it was unlocked.

Widow Saunders appeared to have a passion for gardening. The brick walk was flanked by impeccably trimmed dwarf boxwood hedges. Pansies filled boxwood parterres on either side with vibrant colors. Early blooming sassanqua camellias, limbed up as standards, punctuated the beds. On the steps, stone urns spilled fragrant whips of rosemary in all directions.

The front doors were solid oak and each bore a brass knocker in the shape of a lion's head. Not wanting to announce myself with a bang, I searched until I found the bell, hidden discreetly in the mortar between two bricks.

There should be a book of rules on door answering. Before the advent of voice mail, Ann Landers suggested we all wait ten rings before hanging up a phone. Taking that advice into account, I propose that one at least count to ten before assuming that an unanswered bell means no one is at home. Many is the time I've been indisposed, only to rush through my ablutions to no avail. Not everyone lives within arm's reach of their front door, you know.

Taking my own advice to heart, I counted to ten. *Three* times. Then I rang the bell again. Counting to forty did no good, so I started reciting those bits of Americana I had managed to memorize in school. It was during the preamble to the Declaration of Independence that the door to my left swung wide open. The sudden displacement of air created suction and I found myself hurtling headlong into the maw that was Widow Saunders's foyer. Fortunately for me, my progress was stopped by the belly of a very tall man.

"Oh, excuse me," I blurted as I struggled to get my balance.

"You rang?" he said.

I staggered back a couple of steps and peered up into the stratosphere that surrounded his face. He was a very handsome man. I'm terrible with ages, but I'll guess he was about thirty. His light brown hair was short, although longer in front, and was parted on the side. His eyes were magnolia leaf–green. His skin had the glow that comes from being outdoors upon occasion, but without overdoing it. His body was—well, it was simply divine. If the young man's abs had been any firmer, I would have suffered a concussion.

"I'm here to see Mrs. Saunders." That's what I tried to say at any rate. About the fifth time I got it right.

"Do you have an appointment?"

"I didn't know that was necessary. Say, who are you? Mrs. Saunders's bodyguard?"

"No, ma'am, I'm Caleb. Her secretary."

I smiled ruefully. None of the boys in my typing class had ever looked like that. If Irene Cheng ever quit—or I got up the nerve to fire her—what were the odds I could find a replacement that looked like the beefcake in front of me? A straight beefcake, I mean. And this one was straight, believe me. Pheromones were bouncing every which way in that foyer like lost dogs in a meat market. Okay, so maybe most of the pheromones were mine, but my body doesn't dispense with them freely unless it senses there is a chance for reciprocation.

Yes, I know, I'm engaged to be married, but what difference should that make? I'm constantly having to pick Greg's eyeballs off the sidewalk, so to speak. What's good for the gander is good for the goose, I say—just as long as the goose doesn't goose the gander she's not attached to.

"What's your name, ma'am?"

Ma'am? In a perfect world a stud muffin like that would be calling me Abby, or baby. Not ma'am.

"Abigail *Timberlake*," I said. I hadn't emphasized my last name like that in years. Not that I didn't have a perfect right to do so. Besides two children and a broken heart, a name is all Buford ever really gave me. If throwing his moniker around opened a few doors, then so be it.

The hunk peered down at me, as if noticing the Lilliputian at his feet for the first time. "You're not related to the woman on the news, are you?"

I tried to be patient. "That would depend on which woman you mean. But if you're talking about the one found dead in a suit of armor, the answer is yes, although in a roundabout way. She was married to my ex-husband.

"Anyway, as I understand it, Widow—I mean, Mrs. Saunders is supposed to have quite an armor collection. I was hoping I could get a chance to look at it, maybe make a few notes. I'm an antique dealer, you see, and I thought I could help the police identify the armor you saw on the news."

It took my voice a few seconds to carry up to his cute little ears. Another couple seconds were chewed up as his brain processed my words. I'm not complaining, mind you. Older men have put up with this minor inconvenience since time immemorial.

"Ah," he finally said, "maybe you should speak to Mrs. Saunders."

I bit my tongue. "Lead the way," I said cheerily. I have learned from my friend Magdalena Yoder, up in Pennsylvania, that false cheer can be cultivated, and is an invaluable tool in marketing one's business. Or just getting one's way in general.

"Just a moment, please."

It was a pleasure to watch Caleb trot off to find the mistress. He filled his tight jeans very nicely, and the views, both coming and going, were worth driving across town for. And lest you think I'm going too far in sharing this randy observation, allow me to remind you that we women have historically been on the receiving end of leers. It is time we gave tit for tat. Well, you know what I mean.

"She'll see you in the drawing room," he said, and without further ado led me down a portrait-lined hallway and through a set of open mahogany doors.

I gasped.

13

In front of me was the Rob-Bob's salon. I don't mean their actual salon, of course, but a room that looked like I wish their salon had. These walls were covered in pale pink silk damask. The windows were covered with sheers, but dressed with deep rose drapes, also silk. On the gleaming parquet floor was an Aubusson, whose dominant colors were pink, rose, and a green that perfectly matched young Caleb's eyes. The furniture was rococo with embroidered upholstery, and the gilt was echoed in the elaborate frames of the myriad Impressionist paintings that decked the walls. It was definitely a woman's room. With a credit card and a good man by my side, I could live in a place like that and never go outside.

Then I noticed for the first time that one of the chairs was occupied by a small woman about my mama's age. I realize that may sound hard to believe, but she was wearing a flowered brocade suit that all but matched the furniture. Besides, was it my fault the room was so beautiful?

I gasped again. "Oh."

The woman smiled.

I waited for Caleb to make introductions, but when I looked around, the doors were closed and he wasn't there. Fortunately the woman in the brocade bouquet took the initiative.

"You must be Mrs. Timberlake," she said in the husky voice of a smoker—in this case probably a reformed smoker, since there was no telltale stench in the air. "I'm Corinthia Saunders. Please come in."

I was tempted to curtsy before approaching the fabled Widow Saunders. Lord knows, she deserved one for having such good taste in furnishings. However, the last time I tried to curtsy, it was to an English duchess, and I ended up genuflecting by mistake. There is a difference, you know.

At any rate, the next time I go calling on Charlotte's crème de la crème, I'll wear something besides sweats and tennis shoes. Dressed as I was, I felt utterly unworthy to enter such a splendid room. And just for the record, I did not feel unworthy of meeting the widow. All women are created equal—a few men as well.

The Widow Saunders was an astute woman and sensed my discomfort. A true Southern lady, she saw it as her job to put me at ease.

"I'm on my way to a tea this morning," she said. "Otherwise I live in jeans."

"So does the Pope," I mumbled under my breath. And then drawing on my training as a lady, I walked gracefully forward—well, given the limitations of a badly sprained ankle—and extended my hand. "It's a pleasure to meet you," I said in my best modulated tones.

The widow took my hand and then gestured toward her right. A true Southern lady, I knew she would never presume to ask me about my limp without first being given an entrée.

"Please, have a seat."

I did as bidden, although I had no right to sit on a three-hundred-year old chair in sweat pants from Wal-Mart. It felt like stacking comic books on the Bible. When, after a few seconds, I was not struck by lightning, I gathered the courage to speak.

"Ma'am, you don't know me, and I know I should have called first, but I was wondering if I could get a peek at your armor collection."

She looked me over with the eyes of experience. The rich do not gain their wealth, nor do they hold on to it, by naivete. President Bush may have been flummoxed by a supermarket price scanner, but that was an exceptional case. The Widow Saunders, I'd be willing to bet, has seen the inside of a few groceries. Maybe not Bi-Lo, but surely the upscale Hannaford in South Park.

"Do I understand correctly, Mrs. Timberlake, that you are working with the police?"

"Oh no, ma'am. But I thought I might help them."

The widow shook her head. "He may be cute, but he's dumb as a post."

"Ma'am?"

"Caleb. The young man who showed you in."

I giggled nervously. "Ah yes, your secretary."

Her throaty laugh was anything but patrician. "Caleb is not my secretary. He's my—well, I prefer the old-fashioned term—paramour."

"You don't say!"

She laughed again. Marbles rattling in a jar is what came to mind.

"Oh dear. Mrs. Timberlake, have I shocked you?"

I caught my breath. "Frankly, yes. But not in a bad way, you understand. I mean, you go, girl!"

"So you approve?" She sounded merely curious.

"It isn't my business to approve or disapprove of your romantic life. But I must say that I'm delighted to see a May-December relationship in which the tables are turned. In fact, it's the second one I've seen in two days." I clamped a tiny hand over a very big mouth.

"Don't be embarrassed, Mrs. Timberlake—may I call you Abigail?"

I nodded.

"And please, call me Corie. Anyway, as I was about to say, I have no illusions about the boy. I know he wouldn't look at me twice—what with my wrinkles and wattles—if he didn't think I was loaded."

"I beg your pardon?" I only pretended to be confused. The woman certainly had wattles. For her sake, I hope she stayed indoors the week of Thanksgiving.

"Oh, come off it, child. I'm old. There is no getting around that. And while they're right about money not buying happiness, it can—and in this case, does—buy companionship. And"—she lowered her raspy voice to a whisper—"the best sex I've ever had. *Ever.*"

"Oh, my." I felt the color rush to my cheeks.

"Gracious me, now I've really embarrassed you, haven't I?"

She had, of course, not that it mattered. I would be lucky to even have a sex life when I was her age. Heck, I would be lucky just to reach her age. And while normally I would think this conversation inappropriate for two strangers, I was fascinated by Corie Saunders.

She was doing what rich men have done through the ages. Men like Aristotle Onassis, for instance. And not just really old rich men, either. Does anyone really think Donald Trump could flaunt a progression of beauties on his arm if he were dirt-poor? And would fillies—er, I mean women younger than some horses—trot into Michael Douglas or Jerry Seinfield's stables, if these men worked at Arby's, making roast beef sandwiches for the minimum wage? I think not.

"It's just that I'd rather not hear any details," I said. "If you please."

Corie nodded and reached in the drawer of a small marquetry table of graceful proportions. She withdrew a packet of Virginia Slims and what appeared to be a solid gold cigarette lighter.

"Mind if I smoke?"

"Absolutely."

Corie grinned. "Good. I was hoping you'd keep

me on track. I haven't had a cigarette since, well—
since an hour ago."

I made a point of sniffing the air.

"Ha! You have moxie, Abigail. I like that. Re-
minds me of myself, when I was your age. But to
answer your question, this house has a first-rate
air filtration system. My late husband put it in for
his armor collection. That stuff rusts if you look at
it cross-eyed."

I nodded agreeably. "And speaking of that
armor, Corie"—I must confess here that addressing the fabled woman by her nickname made the
hairs on my arms stand up with pleasure—"may I
please see it?"

"I'm afraid that's impossible."

"No fair," I wailed. "You titillate me by alluding
to your sex life with that stud muffin out there, but
then you're unwilling to let me examine your antiques! What's that all about? You were willing to
show the collection to Rob Goldburg and Bob
Steuben, for crying out loud. Why them, and not
me?"

"Because I no longer own the collection, that's
why."

Thinking I had heard wrong, I shook my head
to clear it of cobwebs. Thank heavens no spiders
fell out.

"What?"

"I sold the entire collection last Monday."

"Why?" I still couldn't believe what I was hearing.

"Abigail, the armor was my husband's passion,

not mine. In fact, I've decided to sell most everything, including this house, and start over again someplace new."

"With *him*?"

She nodded. "Abigail, it isn't easy being an icon. I'm almost seventy years old. I'm tired of shouldering the burdens of my position—a position I never aspired to by the way. So, like I said, I'm starting over. Someplace where I can be just me."

"Where?"

"The Riviera maybe. Not the popular watering holes, of course—I'm likely to run into Charlotteans there. But I was thinking of Genoa."

"Let me get this straight," I said. "You're willing to give up the A-list in the Queen City for Genoa with some gigolo?"

The marbles got a good workout. "Maybe if there was someone like you in my crowd, I'd be tempted to stay put."

"Thanks. I'll take that as a compliment. Corie," I said in my best getting-back-to-business tone, "to whom did you sell the armor collection? If you don't mind my asking?"

"Oh, not at all. It surprises me, however, that you know nothing about the transaction."

"Why should I? Was the sale advertised?" As well as my business is doing, it would still have been a stretch for me to buy a single piece of authentic seventeenth-century armor, much less an entire three-quarter suit. Even had I been able to acquire, say, a helmet and visor, to whom would I sell it? Let's face it, it would have to be an eccentric, or someone with a strong sense of whimsy and money to burn. "Hey," I said, before she could answer my questions, "it wasn't a gentleman by the name of Captain Keffert, was it?"

Corie shook her head.

"It's that Meredith woman! It's got to be. She may not be as eccentric as the so-called captain, but she's rolling in dough. And," I added generously for Corie's benefit, "she, too, has a boy toy."

"Is that so?" The corners of her mouth twitched, causing her wrinkles to dance.

"Oh yes. He's her tennis instructor. Roderick. But he's not as cute as your Caleb." It was a harmless white lie.

I got treated to another concert of marbles in a jar. A long one. If I'd had a kazoo in my purse, we could have made some funky music together.

"Oh please, Abigail," she finally said, "you're too much. But no, it's not Lynne. And yes, my Caleb is cuter."

"You *know* them?"

"Certainly. Lynne and I move in some of the same circles."

"But she's a Yankee!" I wailed. "A Buckeye from Ohio. My ancestors have lived in the Carolinas since before the Revolution and I—well, never mind."

"No, say it." There was definitely a glint in those beady old eyes.

"Okay, but only since you asked me to. I was about to say that I've never moved in any of your circles."

She leaned in my direction and I had the feeling that had I been close enough, she would have patted me. Apparently the woman had a tender side.

"Abigail, please understand that Lynne moves in only some of my circles. The widest ones. She certainly does not number among my intimates."

"Whew, that's a relief."

"Now, now, dear, sarcasm doesn't become you. Besides, after I move to Geneoa I'll have whole new circles to establish. And since I won't know anyone at first, you're welcome to come over and get in on the ground floor. I'm sure I could use a sensible friend like you."

I hoped Corie was teasing. But if she wasn't, I suppose I should have been flattered. Who would have thought a girl from Rock Hill would someday be invited to Europe, to befriend one of Charlotte's elite? Certainly not me.

"That's very generous of you, Corie. If I ever cross the Big Pond, I'll look you up. In the meantime"—I pushed up one of my sweatshirt sleeves to glance at my watch—"would you please tell me who bought your late husband's armor collection?"

Corie settled back in her chair, her hands folded in her lap. Judging by the Cheshire cat grin distorting her features, she was going to relish the disclosure when it finally came.

14

"It was your ex-husband. Buford Timberlake."

If I'd fallen off my chair, I would have cracked my skull wide open on a coffee table. Since coffee tables were not in use in the seventeenth and eighteenth centuries, someone—a recent ancestor, I hope, and not the old dame herself—had converted a Louis XV *bureau-plat* into one. Fortunately I teetered instead of toppled.

"*Buford*? My Buford? Buford the Timber Snake Timberlake?"

She nodded, pleased at my response.

"But he doesn't know the first thing about antiques!"

"I had him out here so I could rewrite my will. You wouldn't believe how tricky it is to exclude blood relatives from inheriting one's estate, especially if one has no intention of marrying one's beneficiary." She waved a liver-spotted hand. "But never mind that. What I'm getting to is that your Timber Snake, as you so charmingly call him, was quite taken with my late husband's collection. So much so, in fact, he made me an offer on the spot."

Perhaps I shouldn't have been surprised. Buford and I once spent a long weekend in the Windy City, during which we visited the Art Institute of Chicago. Whereas I preferred to browse the Flemish masters, Buford was flat-out fascinated by the George F. Harding collection of late medieval and Renaissance armature. I couldn't drag him away from the display. It took two security guards and the threat of arrest to get him out the doors at closing time. Still, there is a big difference between appreciating a finely crafted suit of armor and shelling out the kind of bucks needed to buy an entire collection.

Still, ever since that weekend in Chicago, Buford has displayed an unnatural passion for armadillos, tanks, football helmets, and jockstraps. Never one to do things in a small way, I wouldn't put it past him to buy the widow's collection, but not without consulting an expert first. And just who would that expert have been? One of the Rob-Bobs, that's who! How cagey of them to suggest that Tweetie's metal coffin had been a fine European imitation.

"Drat!" I said, perhaps a bit vehemently.

"I beg your pardon, dear?"

"Oh, nothing."

"But it is something. You look very annoyed."

I sighed. "It's just that the Rob-Bobs—that's what I call Rob Goldburg and Bob Steuben—misled me. I thought they were here to appraise some furniture, or maybe some artwork. They didn't let on at all that they were in on the armor. And they're two of my best friends."

She looked puzzled.

"Rob's the tall handsome one," I added for further clarification. "Dark hair, just turning silver at the temples. Bob's skinny and kind of gawky, but he has a voice that would tame the Bosphorus Straits."

"I know who they are," she assured me. "But they did appraise my furniture. Well, most of it, at any rate. There are a few pieces I'm considering shipping to Genoa, but the bulk of it I've decided to put up for auction in Atlanta. Mr. Goldburg seems to think I'll get more for it there. Charlotteans, he says, are too conservative. Do you agree?"

"Well, uh, are you saying my friends didn't appraise the armor collection?"

"Gracious, no!" The marbles rattled briefly. "I got an armor expert for that."

"Who? If you don't mind my asking."

She studied me closely, which, given my size, only took a few seconds. "A dealer by the name of Wynnell Crawford."

"Get out of town!"

She recoiled, no doubt due to the strength of my ejaculation. "You seem quite excited by this, Abigail."

"Excited? Flabbergasted is more like it! Wynnell couldn't tell a jousting helmet from a tin can. Her specialty is Victorian furniture, for crying out loud. Late Victorian, at that!"

"Perhaps you underestimate the woman."

"I think not! Her shop is called Wooden Wonders for a reason. Virtually everything in it is wood. She doesn't even like to stock tables with marble tops."

"That may be, but I called several of the best museums in the country, and everyone agreed she was the woman to do the job."

"But that's impossible. Wynnell is my very best friend in the entire world—even better than the Rob-Bobs. If she was expert on armor, believe me, I'd know."

"Perhaps it's just something you've never discussed."

"She's my best friend," I wailed. "We discuss everything. Okay, so maybe not *everything*. Otherwise I would have known that Ed was diddling Tweetie, if I may be so vulgar as to use that expression."

Corie stood. She wasn't much taller than I. Then again, she had a number of years on me. By the time I was her age I was going to have to wear stilts whenever I went out, or risk being mistaken for a first-grader by the nearsighted. Thank heavens for wrinkles.

"Mrs. Timberlake," Corie said, her voice colder than a brass bra, "as I said earlier, I have a tea to attend."

I hopped to my feet, too late remembering my ankle. The yelp that escaped these lips was enough to make the stud muffin come running.

"Corie, you all right?"

The grande dame blushed at her consort's public familiarity. "I'm fine. *Mr. Jenkins*, please see Mrs. Timberlake to the door."

"Yes, ma'am." Caleb made the mistake of grabbing one of my elbows. A swift kick to his right shin rectified that.

"Hands off, buster!.

"I didn't touch her, Mrs. Saunders."

"You're a liar," I snarled.

"Hey, you're not worth touching."

"How rude! But then again, you don't know any better, do you?"

"What's that supposed to mean?"

"It means that not only do you look like Adonis, but you have the brains of a statue to boot."

"Bitch."

I gasped. "Did you hear what he just called me?"

The venerable Widow Saunders fixed us both with a look that could have frozen tomatoes to the ground in July. If she ever tired of Genoa, I'm sure Buckingham Palace would be happy to take her in.

She looked pointedly at me. "I am not amused."

I lowered my eyes. "Sorry, ma'am."

"You, Mr. Jenkins," she said addressing her lover, "you and I will talk about this later." With that she sailed regally out of the room

Caleb glared at me. "See what you did?"

"Me? You started it!"

"If that old bat dumps me, you'll pay for it."

"I'm scared stiff, dear—*not*! And just for the record, I hope she does dump you. There have got to be a thousand other gigolos in Charlotte willing to take your place. Although if I were her, I'd wait until I got to Genoa to pick a new one. A nice Italian stallion. Hmm, I might consider a trip myself."

Caleb had the audacity to laugh. "Ha! Well, I wouldn't sleep with you if you were the last woman on earth."

So much for the power of stray pheromones. I hobbled from the room in a huff. I would have slammed the front door behind me when I exited the house, except for one minor detail. As I was passing through the foyer I noticed in my peripheral vision—which is excellent, by the way—that the dining room was to my right, and that the massive table in the middle was loaded with silver. Gobs of silver. I don't recall ever seeing so much of the shiny stuff in one place before. Cutlery, chalices, chafing dishes, candelabra—and not just the C words, either, but sconces, tea sets, picture frames, you name it. I felt like Ali Baba in the forty thieves' favorite hiding place.

I was admiring my reflection in an English punch bowl when I heard footsteps approach from the foyer. What was a greedy gal to do? There were two options as I saw it: I could duck under the table and make like a pedestal, or I could slip into the kitchen. I chose the latter.

Mercifully the institutional-size room was empty of people and I managed to thread my way through the maze of stoves and refrigerators and sundry counters undetected. As I was closing the kitchen door behind me, however, a long black luxury car turned into the driveway and approached the house. I can sometimes think fast on my size fours, if I say so myself, and this was one of those times.

As the car neared, I smiled and waved. Then just as calmly as if I owned the place, I limped down the edge of the driveway, past the car, and out to the street.

When the going gets tough, the tough get going, and the weak go home to their mamas. Especially if the weak are afraid to return to their own homes. My mama lives in Rock Hill, South Carolina, which is over the state line, and used to be a city entire unto itself. It still maintains a strong identity, but during my lifetime the geographical boundaries have blurred; Charlotte has spilled over into Pineville, which in turn has, save for the Anne Close Greenbelt, merged with Fort Mill, which now sits in the lap of Rock Hill. A goodly portion of Rock Hill's population works in Charlotte, and virtually everyone shops there.

At any rate, since Mama is only three inches taller than me, there was a chance one of her dresses might fit. Besides, she has a decent shower and enormous towels of fluffy white Egyptian cotton. And last, but not least, Mama can, if the mood suits her, be downright comforting.

The mood seemed to suit her, and Mama threw her arms around me, and then threw me into the shower. I smelled like a high school kid back from a class trip, she said. While I took advantage of her suds and electric bill, Mama hemmed one of her ubiquitous Donna Reed frocks to fit my shorter frame.

Clothed in a peach and white plaid dress with a full circle skirt poofed up by crinolines, peach pumps, with matching peach hat and gloves, I looked like a mini-Mama. Yes, I know there is an age difference, but Mama colors her hair, and mine has yet to turn. Besides, we both stay out of the sun. Sure, Mama still has a few more wrinkles, but to the casual observer, and from a distance, of say, twenty feet, we looked like two tiny peas in a pod. *Petite Seour*, if you will. The only thing I lacked to make my transformation complete was Mama's signature strand of pearls.

Mama beamed when she saw the slightly smaller version of herself. "I knew it, Abby! I just knew the potential was there. Wait until the ladies at church see the new you. Then we'll see who gets the last laugh."

I frowned in annoyance. "Mama, the ladies at the Episcopal Church of Our Savior will not—over my dead body—get a chance to see me in this getup. This is strictly temporary, until I figure out what to do about my clothes. About my house in general. And what's this about getting the last laugh? Who's laughing, and why?"

Mama turned her pink-and-white back on my peach and white front. "No one's laughing, Abby, but Dorothy Redfern does keep asking when you're going to grow up and start acting like a lady."

"A lady? When have I ever *not* acted like a lady?"

Mama turned just enough to look at me with one eye. "Dorothy says she saw you wearing shorts in Carolina Place Mall. *Without* hose."

"Well, hush my mouth and hope to die. Did she call the fashion police? Because if she did, Dorothy would have been arrested herself. Blue hair and blue eye shadow have been out for years."

Mama faced me. "Go ahead, Abby, and make fun of my friends."

"I'm not making fun of them, Mama. I'm trying to make the point that we each have our own styles, and just because I don't dress like you do, doesn't make me any less of a lady."

Mama sniffed. "Maybe. Oh, Abby, I don't want to argue. Not when we have more important things to talk about."

I hugged her at arm's length. Trust me, I'm not at all adverse to giving Mama a proper hug, but our respective crinolines made it impossible for us to get any closer. An expert on starched slips, she understood.

"Yes, we do have a lot to talk about. For instance, Mama, you're not going to believe this, but I was just in Corie Saunders's house."

Mama blinked.

"The Widow Saunders," I said slowly, so the words could sink in. "Mrs. Gavin Lloyd Saunders."

Mama's first reaction was to turn the color of a perfectly ripe avocado. I'm talking about the inside of the avocado, of course, not the peel. Her second reaction was to gasp so hard she deprived her bedroom of its oxygen and I felt myself go light-headed. Mama's voice, when she finally found it, sounded like it was come to me through a tin can tied to a string.

"Abby, you wouldn't lie to your poor old mama, would you?"

"Of course not, Mama. Why would I do that?"

Mama hung her head. "Because of the Mel Gibson thing."

She was referring to the fact that Mel Gibson filmed a portion of the movie *The Patriot* right here in York County, South Carolina. The production required hundreds of extras, most of whom played the part of Colonial era infantrymen. There were very few roles for women, but Mama claimed she got one of them, as a mature British housewife who seduces Mel in the steamy opening scene.

Why Mama thought she could get away with that claim is beyond me. I happen to think Mel Gibson is a hottie, and I was the first in line to buy a ticket when it premiered in Charlotte. I dragged Mama to the theater with me, kicking and screaming, and complaining of a migraine headache. I should have known something was wrong then, because Mama thinks Mel's hot, too. Imagine my smug disappointment, not to mention her embarrassment, when the opening scene unfolded to reveal very little steam, and not a trace of Mama.

"Yes," I said, "it's the Mel Gibson thing. Can you blame me?"

"Of course not, dear." Mama risked squishing

her crinolines and grabbed my hand. "Abby, were you really in *her* house? Did you get to meet her?"

"Indeed, I did. And Mama, guess what? She sold her armor collection to Buford! And she used Wynnell as her appraiser!"

"That's nice, dear. What was she wearing?"

"Mama!"

"Abby, don't keep me waiting. Is it true she doesn't wear slips?"

"I didn't see her underwear!" I wailed. "I was there on business."

Mama's expression was identical to the one she wore the day my brother Toy left to seek his fortune in California. "Abby, does it always have to be about you?"

I sighed. "Okay, Mama. I'm sure you'll be delighted to know the old biddy has a boy toy named Caleb, and that the two of them will be running off to Genoa, Italy, any day now."

Mama stamped a pink pump. "Shame on you for making fun of your Mama. I endured thirty-four hours of excruciating labor to bring you into this world, and this is the thanks I get?"

"It was thirty-*six* hours, Mama."

"Are you sure?"

"Yes, Mama, I was there, remember? Okay, so I made up that stuff about Widow Saunders and her boy toy. The truth is, I didn't even get to see her. I only met her secretary, who happens to be a woman older than God."

"Really. Oh Abby, describe the secretary!"

I thought of my seventh grade teacher, Mrs.

Turnipseed. "Well, she has thick tortoise shell glasses and she wears her hair in a bun."

Mama shuddered. "What color was her dress?"

"Gray like her hair. Incidentally, Mama, she uses brown bobby pins to hold that ugly bun in place. Can you imagine that?"

Mama smiled. "Oh, Abby, it's going to be so much fun having you live right next door."

"Say *what*?"

"Didn't I tell you? Oh dear, I must have forgotten."

15

orget the crinolines. I would have grabbed Mama by her lapels, had she been wearing any. The last time she "forgot" to tell me something was shortly after I was divorced from Buford. Mama had put a full-page ad in the *Observer*, advertising for a husband—not for her, which would have been bad enough, but for *me*. Little did either of us know that the newspaper is available at specialty stands in every state, and that in every state there resides at least one kook.

"Mountain Man from Montana" wanted to know if I shave my legs, a reasonable question given that he proposed I join him in his unheated cabin at a nose-bleed altitude. "Arnie in Alaska" invited me to run with his dog sled team—in the traces! And just so you don't think all the kooks are from the wilder, or more open, states, "Nick in New York" proposed we get married on the observation deck of the Empire State Building. Nick would dress as King Kong, and I as Faye Wray. And by the way, did I mind being his thirteenth wife?

"What have you so conveniently forgotten to tell me?" I demanded.

Mama smiled coyly. "Louise Melton is selling her house. Plans to move to Texas to be near that no-good daughter of hers. Amber. You remember her, don't you, Abby? Anyway, if you ask me, Louise should have washed her hands of that girl years ago. This is her third drug conviction, you know. Still, I guess somebody has to look after the grandbabies. Lord knows Freddy—that's Amber's husband—isn't fit to take care of the little ones. Last month he was arrested for impersonating a policewoman. A police*woman*."

I borrowed from tomorrow's patience. "That's all very interesting, Mama, but what does that have to do with me?"

Mama's eyes were a study in innocence. "Abby, didn't I tell you?"

"Out with it!" I shrieked.

"Okay, dear, but there's no need to get yourself in a state. This is good news. I convinced Louise to sell it to you direct, which saves her a bundle in Realtor fees, which means a savings for you as well. Plus I got her to agree to a generous allowance for window treatments. Even she knows that those so-called drapes in her living room are uglier than homemade sin."

"You *what*?"

Mama, who has mastered the art of selective hearing, patted her pearls proudly. "Abby, there's no need to thank me, dear. Never mind that I saved you a good ten thousand dollars. How does November thirty sound as a closing date?"

I found myself literally gasping for air. It felt very much like the time Buford held me under the waterfall on our honeymoon. He claimed later it was a joke, but he wasn't amused that the only way I could free myself was to punch him in the family jewels.

"You didn't!" I finally managed to say.

"Oh, Abby, I knew it would thrill you. But I never dreamed you'd be speechless with joy. By the way, while I'm thinking of it, Louise wanted five thousand down as earnest money, so I wrote her a check." Mama put up her hands in a stopping gesture. "There's no need to pay me back right now. Just whenever you get around to it."

"I'll pay you back all right—"

Mercifully, for Mama, the phone rang. I could tell by the delight in her voice that the caller was Greg. After my son, Charlie, Greg is Mama's favorite male, and she dotes on his every word. I had to goad her with the heel of my peach pump—it was a size too big and slipped off easily—to get the phone.

"I want to speak to him when you're done," she said reluctantly and handed me the heavy black rotary phone. The instrument, incidentally, is not a replica, but the real thing.

I flattened my ear against the receiver and turned away from Mama. "Greg?"

"Hey, Babes. You feeling better this morning?"

"As well as can be expected. Under the circumstances."

"Good. Abby, are you sitting down?"

"No, I'm in mama's bedroom. If anyone sits on her bed she gets upset. You know that. Just hates wrinkles on her spread."

"Abby, sit."

"I beg your pardon?"

"Abby, sit on your mother's bed."

"Greg, you like Mama. Why do you want me to tease her?" Lord only knew why I was arguing. Mussing up the woman's covers was the least I could do to pay her back. Heck, that would be only the tip of the iceberg.

Greg couldn't read my mind. "Sit, damn it."

I sat. "Greg, what is it?"

"It's the Widow Saunders," he said gravely.

"What about her? I was just there, you know—"

"That's what I thought. Abby, Mrs. Gavin Lloyd Saunders is dead."

"What? When?"

"Abby, can you meet me for lunch?"

"Well, I suppose—"

"I'm at Bubba's. Get here as quick as you can."

Mama got her phone back.

Bubba's China Gourmet on Pineville Mathews Road may not serve up the best food in the Charlotte metropolitan area, but its dishes rank among the most interesting. Where else can one find stir-fried collard greens, sweet and sour okra, and moo goo gai grits? Adventurous diners may wish to sample General Tsao's possum, or perhaps the Thousand Year Old Crawfish (make sure they're fresh first!). Finicky eaters need not dismay. There is always the dynamite salad bar with all the iceberg lettuce you can eat, and if you're really lucky, Bubba will have gotten it into his head to make lime gelatin squares that day.

Parking is always at a premium, thanks to Bubba's low prices, and I had to the circle the lot for at least ten minutes before finding a space. But since I spotted Greg's car right off, I wasn't worried. Finally a Buckeye family of five waddled out and crammed themselves into a mini-van, leaving me with plenty of room, along with the smug satisfaction that Bubba was beginning to get famous above the Mason-Dixon line.

A faux Asian waitress with bottle-black hair and a Japanese-style kimono pounced on me the second I pushed the greasy door open. "I'm your hostess, Kimberley," she said in far too eager tones. "How many in your party?"

"Two, but it doesn't matter, dear. My boyfriend's already seated."

"Oh, but it does matter. Your name, please?"

"Timberlake," I said crossly. "Look. My fiancé is the hunk sitting right over there, so if you don't mind, I'll just join him."

I started toward Greg, but Kimberley grabbed my elbow. "You need to be seated," she said.

"And you need to let go of my arm."

Kimberley did as she was bidden. "I'm only trying to keep my job," she whined. "Bubba—I mean,

Mr. Jenkins—said I have to take everyone's name and seat them in order of arrival."

"I'm your only arrival at the moment, dear." The door opened and a family of four entered. "Well, I was. And since when has Bubba gotten so particular?"

Kimberley whispered behind a smudged menu. "He's going upscale to capture the South Park market. He plans to change the name to Bubba's Asian Buffet and wants to add a few Thai dishes to the menu. He's already added a couple of Japanese delicacies."

"Oh? Like what?"

"Hush puppy sushi."

"What the heck is that?"

Kimberley talked to her menu again. "They're Mrs. Paul's fish sticks, but he cuts them in half and rebreads the ends so that you can't tell."

I thanked Kimberley for the warning, told her to attend to the waiting party of four, and ducked out of her reach. Greg, who was sipping an iced green tea with lemon stood when he saw me hobbling toward him.

"That was fast." He kissed me before sitting again. "No offense, Abby, but for a moment there I thought you were your mother. What's with the getup?"

"I don't want to go home. Not just yet. And since Mama is almost my size, and has such good taste . . ." I let my voice trail off, hoping to be contradicted.

"Speaking of whom, how is your mama?"

It is a question he asks me every time I see him. I know he's just showing that he cares by asking it, but this time it irked me.

"You just talked to her," I snapped. "She's fine, as you could tell. So fine she went ahead and bought me a house in Rock Hill."

"You're kidding!"

"Well, she made an offer at any rate. But I didn't almost break my neck getting here to talk about her. Tell me about Corie Saunders."

Greg settled back in the booth. "You sure you don't want to order first?"

"Greg!"

He spread his large, strong hands. "Okay. I was on my way over here to eat anyway, and I got a call from Investigator Sharp. She in turn had just gotten a call from Investigator McClendon, who was calling from the Saunders mansion. According to McClendon, you were seen at the house just minutes before her body was discovered. Abby, is this true?"

My head was spinning. "Yes, I was out there to see Widow Saunders, and yes, it must have been just moments before she died, because I drove straight from there to Mama's."

"How long did that take you?"

"Maybe forty minutes. Forty-five at the most."

"And then?"

"And then I took a shower. Then Mama and I argued about clothes, and then we argued about the house she wants me to buy. Then you called. I guess I was at Mama's about half an hour."

He nodded. "That fits in with the witness's report."

"What witness? You mean the boy toy?"

"The chauffeur. He was coming back from getting the car gassed—said the widow had an appointment—when he saw you leave by the kitchen door. What was that about, Abby?"

I had no choice but to tell Greg the entire story. You can bet I left nothing out. To his credit, Greg didn't once interrupt me.

He whistled softly when I finished. "An old lady like that running off with a kid. I don't see it."

I decided to test him. "But what if their ages were reversed?"

He shook his head. "I still don't see it. What would we talk about? She wouldn't know my music. Hell, she probably wouldn't even know what a drive-in was."

I beamed. The guy was a keeper. I needed to remember that.

"Well, I won't run off with a younger man," I promised.

Greg laughed. "Not even with a boy toy like this Caleb guy?"

"Tight buns aren't everything."

Greg beamed like the refurbished lighthouse on Cape Hatteras. For a second I thought the smile was for me.

"Have a seat," he said.

I turned in surprise. Investigator Sharp was standing behind me, looking sharper than ever in a baby blue suit. The column skirt was split so high that if I wore it, my cleavage would show—along with everything else. What, pray tell, do you think the department head would do if the men started dressing like that?

"Hello, Gregory." The pair of well-dressed legs had shed her high girlish voice in favor of what she must have supposed was a sultry one. To me she sounded like Lauren Bacall on steroids.

"Hey, Barb." Greg pointed at me. "You remember Abby, of course."

"Mrs. Timberlake," I said in tones crisper than Bubba's lettuce.

Greg patted the bench beside him. "Have a seat."

The blond flashed me a triumphant look and did what she was bidden. I glared at Greg.

"Well, Abby," Investigator Sharp said, "I see you're going to another costume party."

"*What*?"

"I've been admiring your dress. That fifties retro look is so cute. I have a picture of my grandmother courting in an outfit just like that."

"Your grandmother courted in a Conestoga," I growled.

"Abby!" Greg was not amused.

"Well, she started this." I turned to the woman. "This," I lied, "is my favorite everyday dress. It may look quaint to you, but it allows me to move without exposing my hinney. Besides, not all of us look good in pencil cases."

Greg rolled his eyes helplessly.

Investigator Sharp seemed surprisingly pleased with herself. "Well, shall we get down to business?"

"By all means," I said. "I'd like to hit the salad bar before the Great Wall of Cheddar disappears altogether." I was referring to Bubba's edible centerpiece which is carved fresh daily.

"Good. Abby—"

"Mrs. Timberlake."

"Yes, well, Mrs. Timberlake, I'm afraid you have some explaining to do."

I sat on the edge of my seat. Then again, given my height, that's where I usually sit if I want to cross my legs.

"If you must know, I went to see Widow Saunders about her armor collection. I wanted to see if she had any seventeenth-century pieces I could compare with the suit Tweetie was found in."

Barbie appeared baffled. "Why would you do that?"

"Because if it was really an antique, it would narrow your search. There aren't that many people in Charlotte who could afford such a piece, just for the sake of art. Say, is there any possibility I could take another look at that suit?"

Investigator Sharp frowned. "The armor is evidence. We had our own expert examine it."

"You have a medieval armor expert. Who?"

"Mrs. Timberlake, this is not your concern."

"Is it Wynnell Crawford?"

"Cool it, Abby," Greg muttered.

I chose to ignore my beloved. "Because Wynnell

may, or may not, be the expert she claims, but you have to remember she was the one who found the body."

And yes, I did feel guilty for having suggested my best friend might not be a reliable witness. That she might actually have something to hide. The truth was, though, that Wynnell *had* been hiding a lot of things lately. Who knew what remained to be uncovered?

Tweetie's twin twittered. "We don't use suspects as expert witnesses."

"So she *is* a suspect?"

"That's privileged information."

"Fair enough. Can you at least tell me what your expert determined? Was that genuine period armor?"

"That much I can tell you. It's not real armor."

"You're sure?"

Greg cleared his throat. "Abby, please. Let Barb do her job."

I swallowed my irritation. It was every bit as tasty as Bubba's cooking.

"By all means. Interrogate away."

Investigator Sharp gave her head a triumphant toss. Her natural blond mane grazed my fiancé's cheek, but I could tell by his expression that he didn't mind at all.

"Well, *Mrs.* Timberlake," she said pointedly, "you stated that you paid a visit to Mrs. Gavin Saunders to view her armor collection. Did you think it authentic?"

"I never got to see any. She had an appointment so I had to leave."

"Through the kitchen?"

"Okay, I admit it. That was bad judgment on my part. You see, I got kind of mesmerized by all this silver in the dining room—which I didn't touch, by the way—and then I heard someone coming and I didn't want it to look like I was snooping, so I took the easy way out. But I *didn't* kill anybody. In fact, I don't even know how the widow died."

"Evidently she was poisoned."

"By what?"

"I was hoping you'd tell me. Did the two of you have anything to eat or drink?"

I shook my head. "It would have been lovely to have tea in that salon though. You should have seen it."

"Abby," Greg said gently, "there's no need for sarcasm."

"Sorry," I said. "Look, I don't know why you suspect me. I wouldn't have had the slightest motive. I'd never met the woman before this morning."

Before Barbie could bombard me with her reasons, our waitress appeared. I smiled at her gratefully.

"Hey there."

"Hey, I'm Gina and I'll be your waitress today. The buffet is $4.99 per person. Of course you could order off the menu." She leaned forward and spoke softly. "But I don't advise it."

"Why is that? They too busy back in the kitchen?"

Gina stepped even closer. "You have a better chance of escaping food poisoning if you eat from the buffet. It's already been tested, if you know what I mean."

The three of us nodded. We all ordered the buffet.

Gina removed a stub of a pencil from behind her ear. "Will this be one check?"

"Certainly," I said. "My parents here will be glad to spring for me."

"Abb—" Greg started to chide me but stopped. Something outside our booth had caught his attention.

16

I turned and stared. Had I not had a vision check within the last six months, I wouldn't have believed my peepers.

"It's Lynne Meredith," I gasped, "and her stud muffin!"

Greg took a sip of his green tea, his eyes not leaving the new arrivals. "Funny, but I wouldn't have thought this sort of place would appeal to her."

"It's probably a big mistake," I said. "Maybe they were just driving by and were suddenly so overcome by hunger they couldn't drive another mile."

Barbie reached into a blue suede handbag and took out her stenographer's pad. "Lynne Meredith? Yes, I see here that she was one of the guests at your party, Mrs. Timberlake. I had it on my list to interview her today."

"Now is your chance, then."

I got up and walked over to the buffet. On my way I swung past Meredith's table and gave her a meaningful glare. She had the audacity to smile sweetly back at me. Roderick, her tennis instructor, cum boyfriend, actually winked.

When I returned to the table with my plate loaded with a pinch of everything Bubba had to offer, my two lunch companions were already digging in. Barbie, her mouth bulging with Beijing barbecue, mumbled something about the interview waiting until dessert. I readily agreed.

I was building a dike with my moo goo gai grits to keep the sweet and sour collards away from my Jell-O, when Gina made a surprise appearance. In her hands she held a platter of sizzling delicacies I hadn't seen in the buffet.

"It's for you," she said and plopped it in front of me.

"I didn't order anything. Only the buffet."

Gina, a tall angular girl with a myriad of freckles, jerked her thumb in Lynne Meredith's direction. "She sent it."

"Whatever for?"

Gina shrugged. "Wouldn't say."

I studied the platter. "What is it?"

"Bubba's special poop-poop platter."

"You mean pu-pu?"

"That's not what Bubba calls it."

"Well, please tell the lady thank you."

"Tell her yourself." Gina trotted off to take more orders. Apparently she wasn't big on tips.

I sampled the poop-poop platter, decided it was aptly named, and then did as my waitress instructed. Lynne Meredith's face lit up like a jack-o'-lantern with two candles when she saw me approach.

"Hello Abby," she said warmly. "Have a seat."

Roderick patted the bench beside him.

"No thanks. I just wanted to thank you for the platter."

"You're welcome." Lynne had a smile like Doris Day's. In fact, she looked very much like a fifty-something Doris Day, except that Lynne lacked a waist.

A good Southern girl, I was raised with a modicum of manners and wondered how to segue into the question I wanted to ask. Fortunately, Lynne did it for me.

"I suppose you're wondering," she said, "why I sent you the platter."

"As a matter of fact, I was."

"Are you sure you can't join us?"

Roderick patted the bench again.

I reluctantly sat.

Lynne blessed me with an ear to ear smile. "You see, dear, I'm really quite ashamed of the way I behaved last night."

"You mean fanning the fire with your tail?"

"That, too. Although that was an accident. My intentions were good. No, I'm talking about the way I acted when you so understandably threw us out. I'm afraid I was very rude."

I said nothing. My tongue is even nastier than Bubba's cooking.

"I'm especially ashamed," Lynne said, "about

that Sherman comment. Roderick here really called me on that on."

I gave Roderick a tight smile. He is an extremely good-looking young man, better looking even than Caleb, the Widow Saunders's boy toy. Money may not be able to buy happiness, but it can buy handsomeness.

"My great-great grandfather fought in the Civil War," Roderick said. He didn't say which side, but that much was obvious. Around here "civil war" refers to Bosnia.

"Three of my great-granddaddies fought in the War of Northern Aggression," I said.

Lynne looked like she was about to burst into song. "How fascinating! So anyway, Abby, I also wanted you to know that I didn't mean what I said about taking my business elsewhere."

It was my turn to sing. "You didn't?"

She shook her head, and her golden pageboy locks swayed. Not a single hair broke ranks.

"Abby, I adore doing business with you. And you have such good taste."

"Flattery will get you everywhere," I said. I was being sincere.

"No, I mean it. I've been to all the other shops in town, and they might have some exquisite things, but you have an eye for placement. Why, just look at your home, it's like a magazine spread. Did you decorate it yourself?"

"Well, I—hey!" The fingertips on Roderick's left hand had somehow managed to find their way under my right cheek.

"Excuse me?"

"Oh, I was just about to say that I did some of the decorating." As I spoke I slid my fork off the table and stabbed at the space beside me several times. One of fork thrusts was a direct hit, and Roderick groaned before removed the offending digits. "I'd like to say that I did it all, of course, but that wouldn't be giving credit where credit is due."

"Oh, who helped you?"

"Superior Interiors. They're all the way out in Matthews, but they're the best. Ask for Paul."

She nodded, but the glazed look in her eyes told me she didn't give a hoot. "Abby, I still don't know many people down here, but I feel like you and I are almost friends. That's why I hope you don't mind if I confide something intensely personal."

I squirmed. I was glad to be back in business with the woman again, but I'd rather eat Bubba's poop-poop platter than be privy to some intimate confession. Having the boy toy with the roaming hands beside me made it seem almost sordid.

"Hey," I said brightly, "you know I'd really like to stay and chat, but my friends will think I'm being rude."

I started to get up.

"It's about Tweetie."

I sat down again, but closer to the aisle. "What about her?"

Lynne and Roderick exchanged glances. He cleared his throat.

"I'm a tennis instructor," he said.

"I know that. That's how you and Lynne met."

"Yes, up in Ohio. But shortly after we moved here I got a job at Rivertown Hills Country Club."

"I see." I didn't, of course.

Roderick was undoubtedly used to small minds, because he read mine easily. "I know, you're probably wondering why a man in my position would want to work for a living."

"You said it, dear."

He smiled ruefully. "Lynne is very generous, but I have my pride. I like to pay my way—at least some of the time. And"—he winked again—"it keeps me buff."

"Roderick has gorgeous abs," Lynne purred. "You should feel them."

"Thanks, but no thanks."

"No, go ahead," Roderick said, and turned on the bench so I could cop an easy feel.

I resisted the temptation to run my hands down what appeared to be a washboard stomach. Greg's body is quite enough for me. Never mind that his abs are—well, at least they're not flabby. Still, to be absolutely honest, there was a small part of me that envied these older women their boy toys. An incredibly small part. A much bigger part of me was happy for them, and for women in general. I don't think the need to have a boy toy was an emotionally healthy place to be, but it was nice to see that after thousands of years of men having trophy wives, women were finally getting a chance to make fools out of themselves.

"So Tweetie took lessons from you?" I asked calmly.

"Yeah. In a manner of speaking. She isn't—or should I say, wasn't—cut out for sports."

"Too much bouncing?"

"Yeah, and there was no room to swing."

I nodded somberly. There would have been a time when I would have delighted in that conversation. But now I merely felt sorry for Tweetie. And for Buford.

"Anyway," Lynne said, "this may be one of the nation's fastest-growing cities, but in many ways it is still a small town. I'm sure you'll be hearing rumors about Tweetie and Roderick. We want you to know right now that they're not true."

I raised my right brow. "Oh? What kind of rumors."

Lynne frowned, suddenly nothing at all like Doris Day. "Just rumor."

"About an affair," Roderick said. He laughed. "I never touched her. As you can tell, she wasn't my type."

Lynne's frown produced creases deep enough to plant cotton. "Just what is that supposed to mean?"

"It means it's time for me to skeedaddle," I said breezily. "Que sera sera, and adios."

Investigator Sharp seemed far more interested in chatting with Greg than interrogating me. Under more normal circumstances I might have been jealous—okay, so I was a tad jealous—but mostly I was just grateful to escape the third degree. About the same time I finished my meal Barb announced she was going over to Meredith's table. Greg had to get back to the office anyway, so our little group disbanded.

Before we parted in the parking lot, Greg invited me over to his apartment for a seven o'clock supper. He also made me promise not to do any investigating into Tweetie's death. I made that promise with my eyes closed and crossed, and two sets of fingers crossed behind my back. I tried crossing my toes without first removing my shoes, but couldn't quite do it. I figured I was pretty much covered anyway. Then, as I still had Wynnell's car, and a burning question to ask her, I headed straight for her house.

The Crawfords live on Glenkirk Road, an attractive but settled area. The lots are wooded and the houses have character, as do some of the people. The Crawfords have named their house Fallingwater Too, and while it is only vaguely Frank Lloyd Wright in design, the somewhat boxy structure straddles an honest-to-goodness stream.

I parked Wynnell's car on the street and hoofed across a noisy wooden bridge, half-expecting that at any moment a troll would pop out from underneath and demand payment. I have this Billy Goat Gruff fantasy every time I visit Wynnell, and it's half the fun. This time, however, I was focused on business. There were answers I needed from Wynnell. Answers that were a matter of life and death.

17

Ed Crawford answered the door on the first ring. He was once a tall man, but now is slightly stooped by late middle age and sports a small paunch. His hair is thinning and has just regressed to the point that the B word might be applied. Whatever shot he has at being handsome has been compromised by a scraggly, multicolored beard. This clump of facial hair might serve a useful purpose if Ed had no chin. But he does. At any rate, it was hard to imagine what a young, nubile thing like Tweetie would see in an older man like Ed, beard or no beard. After all, the Crawfords are neither wealthy nor powerful.

"Hey Abby," Ed said. He seemed happy to see me. "Come on in."

There is almost no chance Ed could seduce me, but just to be on the safe side, I declined. "Is Wynnell here?"

"No, she's at the shop."

"On a *Sunday*?" The stream under the house was noisy, and for a second I thought I hadn't heard right. Wynnell is a hard worker, and reasonably competitive, but she never goes to work on the Lord's Day. It's her Southern Baptist upbringing, I suppose.

He shrugged. "That was my reaction exactly. She said it was your fault."

"*Mine?*"

Ed smiled. "Well, aren't you open on Sundays now? Wynnell said she has to keep up with the competition."

I bit my tongue. Wynnell does only a fraction of the business I do. Even a month of Sundays wasn't going to make a difference.

"I'll see her at the shop," I said and started to leave.

"Abby, wait! Please."

I turned. "Look, I know about you and Tweetie. I'm sure the police know by now as well. But I didn't tell them."

He blushed. "It's not that. It's about Wynnell."

"What about her?"

"I love her. Can you help me make her understand that?"

"Hmm, let's see. You love your wife, so you cheat on her—"

"I told her I was sorry. I told her the affair with Tweetie was over."

"Of course it's over! Tweetie is dead."

Ed grimaced. "Yes, she's dead, but it was over before then. Tweetie dumped me Labor Day weekend. I came clean to Wynnell last week when she got back from the cleaners."

"*What?* I understood your affair was a one-night stand."

Ed hung his head. "I had to tell Wynnell that. It would really have broken her heart to hear the truth."

"Just how long had the affair been going on?" I demanded.

Ed's scraggly beard mashed into his chest. "Six months. Give or take a week."

I shook my head. "How terribly thoughtful of you, dear. You have an affair with a young blond bimbo—a faux blond at that—and you think you're sparing your wife by lying some more?"

He looked up. "What do you want me to do? Make a list of all the times?"

"Of course not!"

"Abby, I know you won't believe this, but I'm really sorry. Really, *really* sorry. Wynnell is the best thing that ever happened to me. I realize that now."

"If you're so sorry, Ed, then why don't you show it?"

"What do you mean?"

"Well, for instance, why didn't you come with Wynnell to the party last night?"

"Because I knew Tweetie was going to be there."

"Did Tweetie tell you that?" It was meant as a challenge. Ed's claim that it was over didn't mean squat if they were still in communication.

He blinked. "No, Wynnell told me. She said you told her."

"Oh." I could see now why Wynnell had been so

disappointed in Ed's refusal to come to my party. No doubt she'd wanted to rub Tweetie's face in the Crawfords' reconciliation, no matter how tenuous. Who could blame her?

"So, will you talk to Wynnell?"

"No."

He blinked again. "Was that a no?"

"You better believe it. You two have to work this out yourselves."

He took an anxious step forward, and I took a anxious step back. "But you won't poison her against me, will you?"

"Interesting choice of words. But no, I won't poison her against you. If she still wants you, that's her business. *If*, however, she asks what I would do in her situation—well, the answer is obvious, isn't it? I mean, Buford eventually came to his senses, too, and I didn't take him back."

Ed's sigh of relief was downright pitiful. Even against the background of the babbling brook, it was loud.

"Tell me something," I said. "What is it—I mean, what *was* it—you men saw in Tweetie. They weren't real, you know."

He blushed a second time. Maybe there was hope.

"She made me feel good," he said.

"That's disgusting."

"No, that's not what I meant. She made me feel special."

"Special? Special how?"

"Like I was the only man in the world."

"And Wynnell doesn't make you feel this way?"

He shook his head. "She's always too busy. With the shop—with you. A man needs to feel special."

I turned on a tiny heel and started to leave. Then my irritation got the better of me.

"Do you make her feel special?" I demanded.

"Well—uh, I don't know what to say."

"It's not a million-dollar question, Ed. Do you, or do you not, say or do the things she needs to feel special?"

He said something unintelligible. The running water was starting to get on my nerves.

"Speak up, Ed. I can't hear you."

"I said, it's not the same. I need her to make my meals. To bring me a beer now and then. And to be there when—well, you know. When I'm in the mood."

"You're old enough to make your own damn meals, Ed. You can probably fetch your own beer, too. As for the other, well—it takes two to tango. Maybe you don't light her fire."

He looked shocked.

Perhaps I'd been too rough. "Look, you said before that you really love her. Do you ever tell her that? Because that can go a long way to rekindle passion."

"Of course I've told her that."

"When was the last time?"

"Okay, so maybe it's been a while."

"Tell her every day," I said.

It was time to go.

*   *   *

Wooden Wonders lives up to its name. It's not that the merchandise is so spectacular that makes it remarkable, it's the fact that Wynnell has it stacked to dizzying heights. Chairs atop tables and armoires, small beds on large beds, writing desk on bureaus—just getting from one end of the store to the other is like traversing a maze. It's a wonder even Wynnell knows her way around.

I found my buddy on a stepladder trying to balance a magazine rack on top of a drop-leaf table, which was in turn precariously perched above a mahogany sideboard.

"Ashes, ashes, we all fall down," I said.

"Very funny, Abby." Wynnell made several critical adjustments to her teetering tower and descended. "If you're going to yell at me, do it softly. I have a splitting headache."

"Hangover?"

"Worst I've ever had."

I helped her fold the ladder and lean it against another, more stable, pile. "Why would I yell at you?"

"Because—well, there really is no reason."

I wasn't born yesterday. I wasn't even born in this century.

"Don't give me that," I said, my voice rising. "I want the whole truth and nothing but."

"Okay, okay!" Wynnell had her hands clamped over her ears. "It's just that this Investigator Sharp woman wouldn't give up. Finally I had to tell her the truth."

"*What* truth?"

Wynnell cringed. "Please, Abby. I'm not in the other room."

Taking mercy on my friend I hissed softly. "Spit it out!"

Wynnell looked down at her feet. "I told her about Tweetie."

I struggled with my vocal cords. "What about her?"

"I told her that you hated her."

"But I didn't!"

"You used to. You stood right here in this shop and said, 'I'm going to kill that woman.' "

"But that was *years* ago. Just after she took Buford away from me. Wait a minute—you didn't tell Barbie about that, did you?"

Wynnell nodded. "Abby, she was very persistent."

I was shocked by Wynnell's betrayal. We've been through thick and thin together. There was only one excuse for this breach in friendship etiquette that made any sense.

"You sold me out to save your own skin, didn't you?"

Wynnell looked up, but she didn't have the nerve to look at me. "Abby, it looked really bad for me. I had a motive, and I was alone upstairs where the body was found. Plus, she asked me how I felt about Tweetie's death, and I couldn't lie. Not very well. I told her I was kind of—well, glad."

"So you shifted the blame to me?"

"Abby, *please* understand." Wynnell was pleading like my daughter Susan did when she "borrowed" my car to run off to West Virginia to marry the "only man I'll ever love." Fortunately for Susan I was poor then and the car conked out going up the first mountain. Her one-and-only ditched her for a female biker who stopped to offer aid, and Susan went on to have three more "one-and-only" loves. So far.

"I'm trying to understand, dear. I'm trying to understand why my very best friend in the entire world would sic the fuzz on me."

Wynnell laughed, but not inappropriately. "Abby, you're a hoot. I haven't heard the word 'fuzz' used that way since the sixties. And anyway, you have to admit, you sort of implicated me last night."

"I did."

"You better believe it. When you got back from your interrogation, I felt like a deer standing in the headlights."

I sighed. "Well, we're just going to have to stick together. We *know* neither of us did it. Now we just have to find out who did."

"You're the sleuth, Abby."

"Yeah, some sleuth. I went to ask Widow Saunders if I could take a peek at her husband's armor collection and, to make a long story short, now I'm under suspicion for another murder."

"You're kidding! Whose?"

"The widow herself."

Wynnell backed into a tangle of tables that nearly toppled. "Corie's dead?"

I nodded. "It happened just this morning. Apparently she was poisoned. I had the bad luck of being there just a few minutes earlier."

Wynnell staggered to a tower of chairs, wrestled down the top one, and sat. "She was such a nice woman. I really liked her."

"You knew her well?" I still could hardly believe my best friend was an expert on armor. That she might have been buddies with the crème de la crème of Charlotte society blew my mind.

"Not well, but we hit it off. I particularly like the fact that she had a younger, uh, boyfriend."

"There seems to be a lot of that going around."

The hedgerow eyebrows became one straight line. "Why Abby, you sound envious."

"I'm not!" I wailed. "Greg is all the man I could ever want. It's just that I never would have considered dating a man that much younger. Now everyone's doing it."

The hedgerow broke into clumps while she laughed. "That's why I liked Corie so much. Because she was doing exactly what Ed was doing. With one difference, however; neither Corie nor Caleb was married. No one was getting hurt."

"Did you know she was going to run off with him to Genoa?"

"Absolutely. She was far too excited to keep it secret. She kept telling me to 'hurry up with that damn appraisal.' She couldn't wait to start her new life. Of course she swore me to secrecy, or else I would have told you."

"Of course," I said, perhaps a bit snidely. "But if

she couldn't keep her own secrets, why should you?"

"A promise is a promise, Abby."

"Wynnell, dear, did you also happen to know that Buford was the person to whom she was selling the armor collection?"

My friend paled. "Your Buford?"

"You mean you didn't know?"

She looked away. "Okay, so I knew. Abby, I would have told you, but—"

"But what? But you promised not to tell again?"

"Yeah, something like that."

I stomped a size-four, forgetting yet again my sprain. My cry of pain made Mama, all the way down in Rock Hill, drop her can of spray starch.

"You all right?" Wynnell sounded like she genuinely cared.

"No, I'm not all right. My ankle feels like it's on fire." I hobbled over to Wynnell and made her scoot over. "So what other secrets do you have up your sleeves?"

"Abby, please don't be angry. If you must know, I would have told you—promise or no promise, but I knew it would upset you."

"Subterfuge upsets me."

"Come on, Abby, be absolutely honest. You hate the fact that I was appraising something that Buford bought."

"The man has too much money," I mumbled. "At least half of it should be mine."

"But look at it this way, Abby, the money he

spent on the collection was going to be money Tweetie couldn't have—not that it makes a difference now. But speaking of Buford, where is he?"

"On his way back from Tokyo. At least that's what he claims."

Wynnell stood. I'd made her scoot too far.

"So Abby, what made you want to peek at Corie Saunders's—I mean, Buford's—armor collection?"

"I wanted to study some samples of the real thing. I thought if I could prove that the piece in which Tweetie was found was indeed the real McCoy, it would help the police with their investigation."

My friend shook her head. "That Sharp woman already asked about that. I told her the suit found under your bed wasn't genuine."

"And you're sure about that?"

"Well, it's not like I hung around to get a good look. But Abby, that stuff's expensive. You don't just wear it to a costume party. Besides, there are only three other collectors that I know of in Charlotte, besides the widow, who have real pieces. Two of them were at your party."

18

I gasped. "Who were they?"

"This is supposed to be privileged client/dealer information, you understand. It can't go any further."

"My lips are sealed with concrete."

Wynnell sighed. "Captain Keffert is one of them. He buys mostly small pieces in Europe and brings them back for me to identify. To my knowledge he doesn't have a three-quarter suit of—let's see, from what little I can remember, it was meant to look like early seventeenth-century Italian armature."

"That's right," I said. "The Rob-Bobs have confirmed it."

"They have?" The left hedgerow shot up to meet her hairline.

"Well, not that this piece was genuine. But that it was seventeenth century in style."

She smiled with satisfaction. "They may know a lot, but I didn't think they knew everything."

"Wynnell, I'm going to ask Greg if I can examine the piece. Is there anything—any telltale mark, I should be looking for?"

"You?"

"I'm not an idiot, Wynnell. If you tell me what to look for, I can find it."

"Abby, you've been in this business long enough to know that there are generally lots of subtle clues that one goes by when judging the authenticity of just about anything. It's not like I can just say, 'Look for this, look for that.' You really need the piece in front of you while I list all the possibilities. You need me there to point them out." She rubbed her chin thoughtfully. "But there is one thing a real piece would have that a tourist copy wouldn't."

"What's that, besides a higher price tag?"

"A hole."

"I beg your pardon?"

"It's more of a dent, really. You see, Abby, in the sixteenth century firearms were just beginning to become accurate. This created a market for bullet-proof armor. In order to withstand a bullet, manufacturers made armor much thicker, which in turn made it much heavier. A full suit could weigh as much as eighty pounds. To compensate for the extra weight, combatants began wearing fewer pieces, and concentrated on protecting the abdomen and head. That's why the three-quarter cuirassier became popular—the legs became expendable."

"Ouch!"

"True. But better one's leg than one's liver. At any rate, manufacturers needed to prove that armor was bulletproof, and to do this, they shot at the breastplate point blank. The dent caused by this was the proof mark. Get it?"

"Got it. But what if the bullet went all the way through?"

"Then you didn't buy the piece."

"Duh. So theoretically, if the cuirassier in which you found Tweetie was genuine, there would be a dent somewhere on the breastplate?"

"Yes, that's the most likely spot. But bear in mind, Abby, that the proof mark was exhibited by only the highest quality armor. There were plenty of lesser pieces made. Most warfare still consisted of hand to hand combat with swords or lances."

"I see. Wynnell, you said there were *three* collectors other than the widow who owned authentic pieces. Captain Keffert was one. Who are the other two?"

"Donald and Regina Larkin and—"

"Get out! Geppetto and Pinocchio?"

"A small collection. But as I recall, they have some museum quality pieces."

"Wow!" I was practically, and uncharacteristically, speechless. The Larkins, perhaps in an attempt to hide their Yankee origins, collected primarily Southern pieces. Their brick home in Myers Park was filled with Civil War–era Charleston furniture and period memorabilia of all kinds. The most European thing I'd seen in their house was the cup of French roast coffee they served me on my last visit.

But Wynnell was not through. "I'm counting them as one collector, even though they're really both into it. It's unusual, you know, to find a woman that interested in armor."

My heart was pounding with excitement. "So who's the third?"

"Jerry Wentworth."

"The dice?" I was, of course, referring to his party costume.

"That would be die, Abby, since his wife is not a collector at all. Still"—Wynnell laughed—"the dice are loaded. They can afford the best."

I laughed, too, grateful for the information. When one thought about it, it made sense. Just as the Larkins were trying to bury their unsavory Northern past beneath mountains of antebellum mementos, no doubt Jerry Wentworth was trying to erase his blue collar Carolina past by purchasing expensive European antiques. And not just any old thing, either, but the very symbol of nobility. I wouldn't be surprised to learn that a Wentworth coat of arms, either copied or fabricated, hung in their newly constructed South Park home.

Wynnell laughed a little too long. "So, Abby," she finally said, "you forgive me?"

"For holding out on me?"

"If that's how you choose to look at it."

I sighed. "Sure, I forgive you. But you have to do penance."

The incomparable brows bristled in alarm. "I'm not Catholic, Abby, you know that. I'm not even Episcopal, like you."

"Not that kind of penance! I want you to drive me out to the house so I can pick up my car."

We could hear the door to her shop open, even if we couldn't see it. I have a string of authentic Swiss cow bells dangling from a hook on the back of the front door of the Den of Antiquity. Wynnell, as you might guess, has a set of wooden wind chimes. I hate to admit it but her door opens melodically, whereas my door opens with a clang.

"Abby, I've got customers. Look, you can keep my car all day if you like. I'm not planning on going anywhere."

"Thanks, dear, but it's not just about my car. I need some of my things, and I want to poke around a bit and—well—"

"You're afraid?"

I nodded shamefully.

"Of what? Oh, I get it! That thing about the killer always returning to the scene of the crime, right?"

"Well—"

"Ghosts," someone immediately behind me said. "She's afraid of Tweetie's ghost."

I whirled. As I spun, my wounded foot gave out on me and I lost my balance. Fortunately the interloper was none other than C. J., who just so happens to have a generous middle. My forehead bounced off the woman's stomach and I was upright again. The pain in my foot, however, was excruciating.

"Damn! C. J., don't you believe in announcing yourself?"

The big girl grinned. "Scared you good, Abby, didn't I?"

"You *startled* me," I said irritably. "There's a difference. Wynnell, didn't you see her coming?"

Wynnell shrugged. "I guess I was distracted. I mean, I heard the door open, but I was hoping it was a customer. C. J., did anyone else come in with you? Any customers?"

C. J. shook her head. "Hey you guys, I've asked you to stop calling me C. J. My name's Crystal now."

Our young friend was looking right at me, so I let Wynnell do the eye rolling. The three of us, along with Mama, had recently taken a road trip to Savannah, Georgia. The purpose of our visit was for me to collect an inheritance left me by my late daddy's sister. While in that atmospheric city we'd met a woman named Diamond—a voodoo priestess of sorts—who claimed that C. J. had been gifted with the second sight. The girl's new name was to be Crystal, she said.

I'm sure that sounds like a lot of malarkey to you, too, but C. J. takes it seriously. She may be one of the most intelligent people I know—in terms of raw IQ scores—but her emotional chandelier is missing—well, a crystal or two.

"At any rate, *Crystal*," I said, "it's impolite to sneak up on people."

"Sorry. But I heard what you were talking about and I was anxious to help."

"With what?"

"Well, I'm not doing anything special today, so why don't I drive you over to your house?"

"Makes sense to me," Wynnell said.

It didn't to me. C. J. usually spends her Sunday mornings doing *New York Times* crossword puzzles. Not *solving* them, mind you, but *creating* them.

"C. J.—I mean, Crystal—why aren't you home thinking up brain teasers?"

"They never print them, Abby, so what's the use? They claim they're too difficult."

"That's a shame." I was sincere.

"Yeah, well, the editor at *Pravda* says he might be interested. He's going to let me know for sure next week."

I felt sorry for the kid. It had probably never occurred to her that one can't just translate a crossword puzzle from one language into another.

"Crystal, dear, I hate to tell you this, but translating them into Russian isn't going to work."

"Don't be silly, Abby, I know that. These are new puzzles I wrote in Russian."

"You know Russian?"

C. J. nodded. "Not as good as I know Hungarian—but about on a par with my Hebrew and Greek. Definitely better than my Mandarin Chinese, but not nearly as good as my French, Spanish, and Portuguese."

Wynnell's facial shrubbery shot up, while my jaw dropped. "You're putting us on," I said.

C. J. shook her big blond head. "I speak seventeen languages, Abby. How many do you speak?"

"Uh—at least one."

"Good one, Abby. You see, Granny Ledbetter thought we would get bored with our music lessons if she taught us only in English. When I took up the tuba—"

"You play tuba, too?"

"I play ten musical instruments, Abby. How many do you play?" There was no guile in the big gal's voice.

"Well, uh, I played the kazoo in Mrs. Anderson's third grade class. And I play the radio."

"Very funny, Abby. How about you, Wynnell?"

Wynnell must have done something kind for someone that day. While she was struggling for words the mellifluous tones of the wooden chimes announced a customer.

"Oops, sorry, gotta go!" Wynnell said and skipped off, grateful to be out of C. J.'s grasp.

I had no choice but to accept the girl's offer of transportation.

I fully expected to find my house wrapped in yellow crime scene tape and at least one uni-formed officer patrolling the premises. Much to my disappointment, my house and its environs looked no different than on any other day. But a murder had been committed in my home, for cry-ing out loud. Why didn't it rate the same sort of treatment I'd see other crime scenes receive on the six o'clock news?

Perhaps C. J. really did have the second sight. "Don't feel bad, Abby," she said. "It just means that Greg is satisfied he has all the information he needs."

"It's not Greg who's in charge," I snapped, "but a blond bimbo named Barbie."

We were still in the car, sitting in the driveway. C. J. unbuckled her seat belt and turned to me.

"I know, Abby. I talked to her this morning. I was just trying to make you feel better. You always seem so happy when Greg's name is mentioned. Your face just lights up. My granny gets like that when you say asparagus."

I waved a hand impatiently. "You spoke to Investigator Sharp?"

"Abby, she spoke with everyone who was at the party."

"How do you know?"

"Well, okay, I don't know if she spoke to *everyone*, but your assistant Irene says she spoke with her. The Kefferts said the same thing. And—"

"What did she ask? What did you say?"

"She asked about your relationship with Tweetie, and did I know anyone else who might have had a motive."

"I didn't have a motive to kill Tweetie," I wailed. "It's been at least a year since I stopped hating her."

"That's what I told Ms. Sharp. Only I said it had been eight months. But I told her that you were not a violent person, because if you were, I'd know. It seems that I sort of bring out the worst in people in that regard. A woman back home in Shelby even said she wanted to punch my lights out."

I shrugged. C. J. could get under one's skin, like

chiggers on a raspberry bush, but I had never felt even the slightest bit violent toward her. And I have certainly never felt like striking her.

"Abby," C. J. continued, "I've been thinking."

"Always a dangerous thing," I said with a chuckle.

"Yeah, but this time I've *really* been thinking."

I unbuckled myself. "About?"

"I was thinking maybe someone was trying to frame you."

"*Me?*"

"Well, face it, Abby. You get under people's skin, too."

"I do not—okay, maybe some folk's skin, but if that's the case, they deserve it." I was only kidding, of course. I braced myself within the contours of the bucket seat. "You're not thinking of anyone in particular, are you?"

"Nah—well, there is Irene Cheng."

"She said that?"

"She thinks you're bossy."

"That's because I'm her boss!" I wailed. "Besides, she has a lot of nerve! She's practically taken over my shop."

"You're right, I don't think it's Irene. But maybe it's somebody who thinks you overcharged them for something. Or maybe you promised to sell a client a one-of-a-kind, big ticket item—something really rare—and then turned around and sold it to another for even less because you forgot your promise to the first person. Then maybe when the first person complained, you stuck out your tongue. Then maybe they called you childish, and you began crying like a baby. Then maybe—"

"Crystal, this is beginning to sound like your story."

She blushed. "Well, I was way younger then. It happened over a year ago. My point is, Abby, that you need to stop and consider who your enemies might be."

"Point taken, dear." I got out of her car and she clamored after me.

"Abby, whatever happened to Tweetie's sheep?"

"Beats me." I began a quick reconnoiter of the yard, peering into every shrubby clump and behind every tree. There was no trace of a sheep that I could see, not even a pungent calling card.

"Ooh, Abby, look here," C. J. squealed. She was staring at the camellia bush near the back steps that led up to the kitchen.

I raced to her side.

19

"**I**f that stupid sheep's eaten my bush—"

"Ooh, Abby, it's not that. Look!"

"*Where?*"

C. J. plucked a thin white strip of something dangling from a lower leaf. She thrust so close to my face all I could see were her fingertips. I ducked, lest she pluck out my eyes.

"This is lace, Abby. It came from the bottom of Tweetie's pantaloons."

You have to hand it to a twenty-five year old who knows the P word. I took the bit of lace from my young friend and examined it. She could be right.

"Let's say it is," I said. "So what?"

"Abby, don't you see? This means that Tweetie was killed right here by your back porch and thrown into the camellia bush."

I pushed her gently aside and examined the bush more carefully. *Camellia japonica* have large glossy leaves that are leathery in nature. It is easy to discern structural damage, and with the exception of one bent leaf, there was none.

"Crystal, I don't think she was thrown into the camellia. I don't even think she was killed here. I mean, why would the killer lug her all the way upstairs in that heavy suit of armor? Why not just stash her here in the armor? But you may be on to something anyway. Either Tweetie, or her killer, may have brushed against this camellia-perhaps even roughly, while wearing that Little Bo Peep costume. *Or*," I said, trying not to jump to conclusions, "this little scrap of material was dropped here by a bird, or maybe even the wind blew it over from a neighbor's yard."

C. J. nodded solemnly. "Birds are all the time dropping things. And they're smarter too than most people think. Did you know that ravens drop acorns on highways so that cars will crush the nuts open for them?"

"Actually, I do," I said proudly. Busy as I am, I still manage to read from time to time.

"Now storks, they're the smartest birds. They know just where to deliver the right baby."

"C. J., you can't be serious! That's just a made-up story. Something parents tell their children because they're not comfortable telling the truth."

"I know that, silly. I know where babies come from—*originally*. But sometimes a stork will steal a baby from a home that doesn't deserve to have it, and carry it to one that does. Like what happened to me."

I sat wearily on the bottom step. I was in no hurry to enter my house, and the afternoon sunshine felt good on my face.

"Spill it," I said kindly.

C. J. plonked her big frame down beside mine. "Well, it was like this. Granny said there was this couple in town—that would be Shelby—that already had lots of kids, but they weren't very nice to them. Then they had a little baby girl, and the couple got even meaner. They went off drinking all the time and I—I mean the baby girl—almost starved to death. So one day this stork flew over, saw what was going on, swooped down and wrapped the baby in a tablecloth, and carried it to Granny. And guess who that baby was?"

"Jesus was born in a manger," I said just to pull her chain. "Besides, where would they find three wise men and a virgin in Shelby?"

"Ooh, Abby, that's mean! Besides, that baby was me!"

"I know," I said, and patted her broad back affectionately. The girl never talked about her parents, and once when I questioned her, she said they were dead. Killed in a car accident, I believe. So, it wasn't like that at all. Evidently C. J. had been plucked from an abusive home—not by a stork, I'm sure—and placed in foster care with an old farm lady who was battier than a belfry filled with vampires. No wonder the girl had a sandwich missing from her picnic hamper.

C. J. smiled. "You're my very best friend, Abby, you know that?"

"You're a dear sweet friend, too," I said and stood. It was time to get the show on the road before she asked me to be more specific. Wynnell

Crawford would always be my *very* best friend, unless—well, it was silly to even continue that thought. There was no way on God's green earth my bushy-browed buddy was a cold-blooded killer.

The house was cool and darker than I remembered. I flipped on the nearest kitchen light. A few stunned seconds later, I gasped.

"What is it?" C. J. demanded. She had her fists clenched, ready to defend us against an assailant.

"Just look," I cried.

C. J. spun in a full circle, nearly knocking me over. "I don't see anybody. Did they run from the room?"

"It's not a person." I waved my arms. "It's this. The place is spotless!"

"Abby, don't scare me like that. A clean kitchen isn't dangerous."

"But don't you get it? Last night when I left to go to the Rob-Bobs, the place was a mess. Someone washed all the dishes." I glanced down at the floor. "Oh my God, they've even mopped."

"Abby, you're not making a lick of sense."

Talk about the pot calling the kettle black, even though now they were both clean. "I wonder who it was?"

"Ooh, I bet it was your mama."

"Not bloody likely, dear. If it was mama, we'd have read about it in the *Charlotte Observer* first, along with her account of how she endured thirty-six hours of agonizing labor for me."

"Good one, Abby. But no matter who did it, I guess you should be happy, huh?"

I shivered. "I guess so—unless the person responsible for this was the same person who killed Tweetie. I mean, maybe they were trying to cover something up."

Apparently bigger people have less to fear, because C. J. had wandered off into the dining room. "Hey Abby," she called, "why do you have all the drapes pulled?"

So that was it! That's why the place was so dark. The plantation shutters in the kitchen were closed as well. Silly me, indeed. I'd completely forgotten.

"Ah," I said, as it came back to me. "That was Pinocchio—er, I mean Regina Larkin's idea. She said it would be inviting trouble if any of the hoi polloi drove by and saw so many high-profile guests cavorting in one place."

C. J. returned to the kitchen. "She said that?"

"Well, maybe she didn't use the word 'cavorting,' but that's what y'all did. Anyway, she definitely said 'hoi polloi.' "

"Abby, I don't think the hoi polloi drive down your street."

"Maybe not. But it seemed like a good idea at the time. I didn't invite many neighbors, and there was no point in making them jealous."

C. J. nodded. "That part makes sense. People are always jealous of me."

I decided, in the interest of time, not to comment. "Dmitri must be mad at me," I said by way of diversion. "Any other day he would be rubbing up against my legs, meowing his head off to be picked up."

C. J. nodded again. "Just like my cousin Alvin Ledbetter. Except he used to nip my ankles—"

I bolted into the dining room. The powder-blue French silk drapes in that room have a double lining and are surprisingly heavy and utterly opaque. Between the drapes and the window there are enough sheers to blanket half of Charlotte. Until I flipped the chandelier switch, the room was as dark as Buford's heart the day he left me for Tweetie. I pulled hard on the drapery cord and the afternoon sun flooded the room with glorious diffused light.

"Ah, that's much better. Dmitri! Dmitri, where are you?"

True to his heritage, my ten-pound bundle of joy refused to answer. "I'll look upstairs," C. J. volunteered, and bounded up the steps like the African springboks I'd seen in *National Geographic*.

I hobbled on to the living room, the scene of last night's debacle. When I pulled the drapes in that room I couldn't help but groan. The scorched area on the carpet was even larger than I remembered, and if the manufacturer couldn't match the dye lot, the entire floor was going to have to be recovered. Leave it to me to buy the most expensive carpet on the market. According to the salesman it was supposed to last a lifetime under normal foot traffic. He hadn't, alas, mentioned anything about the Statue of Liberty dropping her torch.

"Abby!" C. J. called, rescuing me from my

reverie of needless dollars spent. "Dmitri's upstairs."

I took the steps one at the time. Even without an injured foot, a woman of my stature does not bound like a gazelle.

C. J. waited for me at the top of the stairs. "He's under your bed," she said. "He's acting weird."

I shivered. I'd been hoping to work my way slowly into that room.

"Weird? How?"

"He's rolling around with his feet in the air. And growling, too. Granny Ledbetter used to do that every spring. But it's fall now, Abby. I think something is wrong."

I took a deep breath and charged the scene of the crime. When faced with a flight-or-fight situation, I sometimes surprise myself by barreling headlong into danger, especially if a loved one is involved. And next to my son Charlie and Greg, my yellow tom is the male I love most in the world. Even my brother, Toy, takes a backseat to my four-legged friend. I know, despite his name, Toy is a human being and should count for more than a cat, but Dmitri didn't tease me mercilessly from the moment he could talk. Nor is Dmitri the undeserving apple of Mama's eye.

C. J was right. Dmitri was rolling around like nobody's business and in the exact spot where Tweetie's corpse had been found. It was downright unseemly. Bizarre even.

"Stop that!" I commanded.

Dmitri stopped just long enough to give me a challenging look through green slits, and then went right back to rolling. In cat years my feline is probably older than I, but he often acts like a teenager.

"What do you think it could be?" C. J. asked. "Ooh, Abby, you don't think he's been possessed, do you?"

"Possessed? You mean by Tweetie's ghost?" I couldn't quite suppress a chuckle.

"It happens to animals, you know," the big gal said defensively. "Especially to cats. Granny Ledbetter had a big old Persian that was born on the day Elvis Presley died. So that's what Granny named him. Anyway, even when he was a kitten, Elvis used to go up to Granny's beagle, who was named Darwin, and start to meow something pitiful. This would make Darwin real mad, and he'd chase Elvis all over the place."

"Crystal," I said patiently, "cats and dogs fight. That's what they do."

"But don't you get it, Abby? Granny's cat Elvis was meowing 'You Ain't Nothing But a Hound Dog.' "

I groaned. "Well, Dmitri isn't possessed, and he's for sure not Elvis."

"That's right, but he could be Buddy Holly."

"Somehow I don't think so. Besides, he isn't even meowing, he's just rolling."

"Buddy didn't sing all the time, Abby. Ask for a sign."

I sighed. Anything to shut the girl up.

"Dmitri, if you're Buddy Holly—or anything at all except a cat—give me a sign."

A split second later my doorbell rang. The instrument has four tones, and at the sound of the first chime I did a remarkable impression of a springbok. I didn't intentionally leap into C. J.'s arms, but that's where the second chime found me. By the third chime Dmitri was in my arms. C. J., bless her heart, had no one to leap on.

The three of us trembled with fear. It was all so silly of course, because doorbells rarely hurt anyone. Finally, C. J. came to her senses.

"It still counts, Abby, even if it is a doorbell. Dmitri is really Buddy Holly."

"Dmitri is a cat who still has his back claws," I growled. "C. J., put me down."

"Not until you admit the truth."

"Crystal! Put me down, you big galoot!"

C. J. promptly dropped me. I landed on my injured ankle, and promptly dropped Dmitri. The poor dear was not amused and raced down the hall like he had a pack of hounds after him. Maybe Dmitri was Elvis. Then again, maybe he was just a cat. One thing was for sure; the doorbell needed answering.

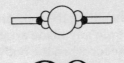

20

My first reaction was to tense up when I saw that the caller was Malcolm Biddle. Then I remembered that just this morning I had elevated him from his position at the bottom of the male pond to somewhere near the surface. Maybe a floating layer of algae.

"Come in," I said, and graciously hobbled aside.

As he passed I noted that his was a rather cute derriere. I directed him to sit on the far side of the living room, so I could ogle his booty a few seconds longer. After all, it wasn't like I was married, and I certainly didn't plan to touch.

"Abby," he said, once we were both seated, "Buford just called. He asked me to give you a message."

"What? He's supposed to be on a plane somewhere over the Pacific."

"He is. He tried calling you here and at your Mother's, and when he couldn't get you, he called me. He has some ideas for the funeral."

I swallowed. "What does this have to do with me?"

"Well, I'll be handling the legal end until Buford gets in, and I've already made arrangements with the funeral home for when the body gets released. But Buford wanted somebody to see to the spiritual side."

"You've lost me."

At that point C. J. clambered into the room. Mercifully she took a seat without being told. I reluctantly made introductions.

Malcolm crossed his legs seductively, one sturdy ankle balanced across the opposing knee. I dared not even glance below his belt.

"Abby, Buford wants you to contact his clergyman. Make tentative arrangements for the funeral. I spoke to a Ms. Sharp on my cell phone on the way over here, and I think we can get the body released in time for a funeral on Wednesday."

"What's the rush?"

I got the impression that Malcolm squirmed, although I swear he didn't even blink. "Buford has a court case Thursday."

"I see. So he's delegating the dirty work."

C. J. gasped. "Abby, we're talking about a friend's funeral."

"She wasn't quite a friend," I said through clenched teeth.

Malcolm smiled. "Abby, I know this has to be tough on you, but Buford didn't know who else to call. I suppose I could handle the funeral arrangements, but I've never done that before. Besides, I don't go to church. I wouldn't know how it's done."

I bristled. "You're not suggesting that Buford wants the funeral held at my church, are you?"

"Oh no. At least I don't think so. He was quite specific about the place. He said Holy Blossom Interfaith House of Prayer on Park Road. That isn't your church, is it?"

"Gracious, no! I've never even heard of the place." Frankly, I was flabbergasted. To my knowledge Buford had refused to set as much as one hairy toe in the doorway of any church following our wedding day, with the exception of weddings and funerals relating to big-name clients. Even our children's baptisms went ignored by him. When he married Tweetie Bird it was at a justice of the peace in Las Vegas.

"Ooh, ooh," C. J. squealed and waved her arm like an inept school girl who finally got one answer right. "Holy Blossom is my church!"

That astounded me as well. I couldn't recall her ever having mentioned a church. In fact, I had the distinct impression she was against organized religion of any kind.

"Since when, dear?" I asked gently.

"Abby, I've been going there for years." C. J. was gazing with adoration upon Malcolm Biddle's comely features. He, in turn, looked like a Crusader who had just found the Holy Grail. My, but that pair moved fast!

"C. J., you've only lived in Charlotte for two years. Before that you lived in Shelby."

"Okay, so it's been two years. But that's still years."

"Just barely. What kind of a church is Holy Blossom?"

"Well, like Mr. Biddle said, it's an interfaith church. Although we don't use the word 'church,' on account of that has connotations. Anyway, what makes Holy Blossom so special is that we accept people from all backgrounds."

"Most churches do, dear."

"Yeah, but at Holy Blossom we try not to judge."

Touché. "Did you know Buford and Tweetie were members?"

"Of course, silly. They came almost every Wednesday—at Holy Blossom we have our services on Wednesday evenings because it's more inclusive."

"You don't say. Well, maybe you should be the one to arrange Tweetie's funeral. You know the pastor, don't you?"

"I'd be happy to, Abby. Sister Deidre is a good friend of mine."

I stood. "Well, I guess that's settled then."

Neither C. J. nor Malcolm seemed to have heard me. They were still giving each other the eye, and the stream of pheromones passing between them was so thick, I could have cut the flow with a knife.

"Ahem," I said. "I've got things to do."

"Go ahead, Abby," C. J. said. "We won't get in the way."

"You've only just met, for crying out loud."

"Maybe it's kismet," Malcolm said.

"Kismet?" I asked incredulously. I couldn't believe a real lawyer would talk that way. Buford should take another look at his colleague's license. Malcolm wouldn't be the first faux lawyer to have taken his bar exam in a tavern.

C. J. nodded vigorously. "Granny always said this could happen."

"What? That you'd make a fool of yourself?" Perhaps I was being harsh, but I care about the girl.

C. J. was on her feet in a flash. She whisked me, stumbling, into the dining room.

"Make fun of me if you want to, Abby, but this could be love at first sight."

"Crystal, you're supposed to have the *second* sight. You should know better than to think two people could fall in love in less than a minute."

C. J. lowered her massive head and trained her eyes intently on mine. "You should be happy for me, Abby—not jealous. You already have Greg."

"I'm not jealous!" I stamped my foot, then howled with pain. I may even have used a few expletives.

"Honestly, Abby, you don't have to be so rude."

"Out!" I said pointing to the door.

"But Abby, I gave you a ride."

It may have been only my imagination, but it seemed to me that her sigh rustled the heavy French drapes. Mama's sighs, I'll have you know, can quiver my curtains all the way from Rock Hill.

"Yes, you very kindly gave me a ride," I said, "and I thank you for it. Look, C. J., I'm sorry if you think I was rude. It's just that I'm feeling incredibly stressed. And all this talk about love at first sight is—well, let's just say it's adding to my stress."

"I forgive you," C. J. said, and there wasn't a hint of sarcasm or resentment in her voice. She looked longingly toward the living room. "Abby, if it's really all right with you, maybe I will go. If you think you'll be all okay here alone."

"I'll be fine." I meant it. The nonsense with C. J. and Malcolm had somehow diffused the spooky feeling I'd gotten upon entering the house.

My young friend patted me on the back. It was supposed to be an act of tenderness, but the gal has huge mitts and the strength of a grizzly bear. It was all I could do to remain upright.

"Take care, Abby. And if you start to get depressed, my granny has a wonderful hot toddy recipe I'm sure she won't mind if I share. It contains St. John's wort, cod liver oil, crème de menthe—"

"Thanks, dear. I'll keep that mind."

It was actually with some relief that I ushered the pair of fledgling lovebirds to the door.

Okay, to be absolutely honest, the second the front door shut behind C. J. and Malcolm, the relief I felt at their departure vanished. It was replaced with an almost overwhelming feeling of doom. Something horrible had happened in that house, and something just as horrible was about to happen again. My instinct was to grab my pocketbook from the kitchen counter and race out of there like a kid on the last day of school. One thing I knew already, there was no cotton-picking way I was ever again going to be happy living in that house.

There were things to be done, however, so I had no choice but to haul myself upstairs one more time. Dmitri, wouldn't you know, was back to rolling around on my bedroom floor. I let him indulge in this strange obsession while I made a quick check of the second-story rooms. Nothing appeared to be missing, and there was no sign of a struggle. The bed Wynnell had crashed on the evening before was still rumpled, but that was to be expected. Apparently the kitchen fairy didn't climb stairs.

Having found no clues in my cursory search, I packed an overnight case with a few essentials, gathered up a complaining cat, and hit the road to Mama's. The unremitting howling of my male companion made the trip almost unbearable. I'm sure you'd think ill of me if I told you I almost stopped at the South Carolina welcome station to let him out—permanently out—so I won't tell you that. I mean, I love the big lug, I really do, but there's only so much a body can take. He may be a yellow-orange tabby, but there's a touch of Siamese in there somewhere, so he has the lungs of a two-year-old human. At any rate, it wasn't until I was a block from Mama's that he shut up long enough to cough up a hairball on the passenger side seat.

Then my luck changed abruptly. As I pulled into my petite progenitress's driveway, I noticed she wasn't home. It's not that I didn't want to see Mama, mind you, but I had important matters to attend to. Playing Scrabble and sipping sweet tea would have to wait for a Sunday afternoon during which I had no murders to solve.

Dmitri adores Mama, and she him. In no time at all he'd settled himself on Mama's pillow and was fast asleep. While he was bedding down I stashed the overnight bag in Mama's best guest room—Toy's old room—and wrote her a short note. I explained that her heart's fondest desire was only temporarily being met, and under no circumstances should she interpret that as my agreeing to buy the house next door.

I grabbed a diet soda before leaving and had one sore foot outside the door when the phone rang. While I don't claim to have C. J.'s second sight, or Mama's nose for sniffing out trouble, there are times when I just know the phone is for me. This was one of those times.

"Hello," I said cautiously. Just because the call was for me didn't mean I'd want to take it.

"Abby, thank God you're there," Greg said.

"Just barely, dear. In fact, I was just leaving."

"Abby, please, hear me out."

I'd picked up the phone nearest the door. It was on a doily on a walnut phone table between a pair of 1950s-style overstuffed armchairs. I hoisted myself into the closest chair.

"Spill it, dear." Just between you and me, I was expecting a lecture on how to be more civil to Investigator Sharp.

"Uh—I don't know how to say this, Abby."

His tone made me uneasy. God forbid I had pushed him too far—right into the skinny arms of his new coworker.

"Just say it. I can take it." I didn't know that I could, but I wasn't about to come across as weak at a moment like this.

"Abby, this is something I should have told you before. And I was going to tell you tonight, at supper, but news like this has a way of spreading like a gasoline fire. I wanted you to hear it from me first."

"Then tell me!" I wailed. My anxiety was so high by then that I was in danger of exploding and starting my own fire.

"Okay, it's like this. I quit my job."

My gasp informed me that Mama didn't dust her house as regularly as she claimed. "When? Why?"

"I gave my notice on Friday."

"But that can't be! You've been tagging along with Investigator Sharp like she was your bosom buddy—no pun intended."

During the ensuing silence a lasting peace descended upon the Middle East and Dennis Rodman grew up. Finally I could take it no more.

"Say something! Anything!"

"Abby, I lied."

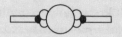

21

"Oh my God, you didn't quit, did you? You're having an affair with Barbie!" My heart was beating so hard I wouldn't have been surprised if it had torn through my chest.

"Damn it, Abby, don't you trust me?"

"Yes, but—"

"When I said I lied, I meant I gave you the impression that I quit this past Friday. But the truth is, I turned in my resignation over two weeks ago. Friday was my last day. That's why I'm not working on Tweetie's case."

I took several deep breaths, willing my heart to slow to a reasonable pace. I read somewhere that the elephant and the shrew, the largest and smallest animals respectively, have the same number of heartbeats. The shrew's heart beats extraordinarily fast and it lives only two years, whereas the elephant, with less frenetic beats, lives half a century.

"Why did you quit, Greg?" I asked with commendable calmness.

"You know what it is I've always wanted to do?"

I took a stab at the wildest fantasy I could remember Greg ever having shared. "You want to
work on a shrimp boat."

"Bingo."

"That's *it*? You quit to work on a shrimp boat?"
It was coming back to me now. Greg had spent his
summers on the coast while growing up, and after
college had served briefly in the merchant
marines. I'd heard of the sea getting to people's
blood, like some mysterious, impossible-to-kill
disease. Perhaps the love of my life had become in-
fected as a youth.

"Abby, I'm forty-seven. I know I've been with
the Charlotte Police Department less than fifteen
years, and I won't be getting any retirement, but
hell, I'd like to do what really makes me happy. I
know this sounds corny, Abby, but I want to look
for my joy. You understand, don't you?"

I did, and I didn't. Greg had joined the department later in life than most cadets. After the merchant marines, he worked for many years as an
insurance adjuster. The career changes were his
choice. I, on the other hand, had become an antique dealer out of necessity. Dealing was just a
hobby with me when Buford traded me in for
Tweetie. An enjoyable hobby, yes, but hardly one
intended as a career. If I were to "look for my joy"
I wouldn't quite know where to begin. Surely not
surrounded by other folk's castoffs.

"This means a move to the coast," I said, thinking aloud. "Where?"

"You remember my cousins, Skeeter and Bo?"

"You may have mentioned them, but I never met them."

"Sure you did. At the reunion I took you to last year. Anyway, Skeeter and Bo own a shrimp trawler that operates from Mount Pleasant, South Carolina. That's just outside of Charleston—"

"I know where it is," I said dryly. "It's a long way from here."

"Abby, darling"—Greg reserved the D word for special occasions—"I was thinking you would come with me."

"You're kidding? Aren't you?"

"No, babes. I wouldn't be making much, but if we're tight, we could live off my salary. But I don't think we'd have to, because you could keep your shop up here. Irene seems to be working out, doesn't she?"

"Yes, but—"

"And if you really wanted to, you could sell the Den of Antiquity and open up a new shop in Charleston."

He made it sound so easy. First a shop here, then a shop there . . . an antique business might sound portable, but it's not. A business, any business, depends on its clientele base, and this must be built from the ground up. Often very slowly. A new shop, however, wasn't the only issue.

"What about Mama? It'll kill her if I move away."

"Sweetheart, Charleston is only three and a half hours from Charlotte. It isn't Timbuktu. Besides, I adore your mother. Why not just take her with you?"

Now he was being ridiculous. "Mama would rather you rip her heart out through her throat than move. I bet she'd even sell her pearls first."

"It doesn't hurt to ask her."

I tried to wrap my mind around all the ramifications of Greg's decision. "What if I don't want to move to the coast?"

He was silent for a minute. "Then I won't go."

"What did you say?"

"There's got to be something I can do around Charlotte. Abby, I may be over the hill, but I'm still damn near the top."

"But happened to following your joy?" I didn't mean to sound sarcastic.

He didn't pause a beat. "You're my first joy, Abby. Shrimping would have been my second. I figure that even if I end up taking a job packing groceries at Food Lion, I'm luckier than ninety percent of the men I know."

That touched my heart like nothing had since the birth of my children, and both floodgates opened. Thank heavens they were silent.

"That's the nicest thing anyone has ever said, dear."

"I mean every word, Abby."

"Stop it," I said, my voice breaking. I dabbed at my face with the hem of my borrowed peach-and-white skirt, leaving huge smudges of Maybelline's Very Black mascara. And just as a word of caution, be careful dabbing when wearing crinolines. I caught a bunch of the stiff material in with the skirt and gave my left eye a good poke.

"You're the most important thing in the world to me, Abby."

"I love you, too!" I wailed.

The truth be known, I'd always had a hankering to live near the beach. When I was ten, before Daddy died, we spent the summer on Pawley's Island with relatives. I remember learning to dance the shag, on clean white sand, to beach music played on cousin Annie's transistor radio. Close to shore, but too far out to reach, dolphins cavorted. Those were simple times when happiness meant rinsing all the sand out of my suit, or helping myself to the unlimited supply of Popsicles in cousin Annie's freezer. The days were long, hot, and glittering. The nights glittered, too, with stars the size and brilliance of the Austrian crystals on the chandelier that now hangs in my home. The beach music still echoes in my brain.

But if I were to move to the coast, it would no longer be to the beach itself. Time has redefined my tastes and needs, and I require more than Popsicles and a sandless crotch. If I were to give up the Den of Antiquity in Charlotte, and leave my friends as well, it would have to be for a historic home in downtown Charleston, in the very thick of things. The sand and Popsicles would be mine on weekends.

"I'll broach the idea to Mama," I said cautiously. "I won't consider moving unless she comes, too."

He sucked his breath in sharply. "You mean it? You're really considering the move?"

"To Charleston, yes. Somewhere south of Broad Street."

He sighed. "But Abby, I hear those houses are very expensive."

"They'd better be. At this age I don't want to live where just anybody can afford to be."

"Damn it, Abby, you've made me the happiest man in the world."

"It isn't final," I warned. "Remember Mama. She's got her church, her friends, her Apathia Club, this house where she lived with Daddy—it's going to be a hard sell."

"You can do it, Abby."

His tone suggested that he might not have been content with his first joy alone. On the other hand, perhaps I was being too sensitive. I decided to cut him some slack. After all, I had some business that needing attending to, if my next home wasn't going to be behind bars. A change of subject was in order.

"Greg, I know you're off the force and all, but I don't suppose there's any way—any way at all— that you can fix it so I can get a peek at that armor. The suit Tweetie died in."

"Sorry, Abby, but I really don't think that's feasible. Besides—and don't go getting your knickers in a knot—do you really think you could tell if it was authentic? I mean, armor isn't exactly your specialty."

"Says who?" I snapped.

He sighed. "Hon, you can't be expected to know everything."

"Well, I know enough to look for a little round dent somewhere on the breastplate." There was no need to share with Greg just how new that knowledge was.

He was silent for a minute. "There was a dent. Forensics determined it was made by some sort of percussion weapon, but one that doesn't match anything out there now. And since the bullet didn't penetrate the armor, and there was no corresponding wound on the body, they decided to leave that hot potato alone."

"That hot potato," I said dryly, "was made in the late sixteen hundreds by the manufacturer. It was his mark of assurance that armor was bulletproof."

"Gee, Abby, you really do know this stuff."

"I have my sources," I said smugly.

"Sorry about that comment earlier."

"No problemo. So, you saw the mark yourself, did you?"

"Yeah. Hey, you don't mind if I pass this on to Investigator Sharp, do you?"

"Go right ahead." Discovering that I had a brain would, no doubt, set the bossy blond's teeth on edge.

"Thanks. Hey, we still on for seven o'clock?"

"Absolutely."

I hung up, feeling more optimistic than I had since before the party.

*   *   *

After hanging up the phone my first order of business was to shed Mama's dress in favor of the jeans and T-shirt I'd packed in the overnight bag. Crinolines and stiletto heels are not practical sleuthing attire, not unless one is on the sound stage of a *Leave It to Beaver* reunion. Properly attired, I headed straight for the Keffert mansion.

The couple lives in Belmont, North Carolina, on the upper reaches of Lake Wylie. Their house is a stucco replica of the *Queen Mary*, and although not quite as large, is every bit as impressive. While I would never live in such a bizarre abode, I will admit that it has some interesting features. The three giant smokestacks function as fireplace chimneys, the lifeboats serve as oversize hanging flower baskets, and the hundreds of portholes let in bright Carolina sunshine. Plus the retractable gangway is an effective security measure.

The Ship of Fools, as it was originally called, has graced the cover of *Architectural Digest, Life, People,* and innumerable smaller publications. The Kefferts' neighbors, rather than abhorring this monstrosity in the middle of their upscale subdivision, are rather proud of the distinction it lends their community. "We live near the boat," they are reportedly fond of saying. Sure, there are a few dissenters, but nobody living on the Kefferts' street can deny that there is at least one advantage in living so close to the stucco ship: both the police and fire departments know exactly where to find them. Even pizza deliveries have improved.

The gangway was up when I pulled into the

navy-blue concrete driveway and parked in the shade of an exceptionally handsome crape myrtle tree. From previous visits I knew to press a button cleverly hidden in a stout pier piling. The resulting blast of the ship's horn made me jump, and I winced with pain.

I refrained from pressing the button again and waited patiently. After a few minutes Mrs. Keffert— or First Mate Keffert, as she likes to be called— appeared on the lowest deck. She had a pair of binoculars in her hands which she tried to focus on me. I could tell she was having trouble, because they bobbed around like flotsam in a turbulent sea of jetsam. Finally she gave up and hung them around her wrinkled brown neck.

"Oh, it's only you," she said, as if she hadn't recognized me from the start.

"Good afternoon, First Mate Keffert," I called, my voice ringing with false cheer. "Is the captain in?"

"He's busy."

"This will only take a minute. May I come up?"

"Mrs. Timberlake, I fail to understand why I should invite you up when you couldn't be bothered to invite us to your party."

"Oh, didn't I invite you to the most fabulous Halloween party of the decade?" I shouted. "What a shame. Why *everyone* who was *anyone* was there."

My ploy worked. Quicker than Rapunzel could let down her hair, First Mate Keffert lowered the gangway. "Come up!" she barked.

I hobbled up the swaying metal walk. The second my injured foot touched the deck, the elderly woman grabbed me by both arms and literally dragged me to the doorway.

"Get inside!" she hissed.

I gasped, but not from pain. I gasp each time I see the Kefferts' salon. Their decorating scene isn't nautical in the least, but a bewildering collection of curios amassed through their life's voyage together. For instance, there was a real, but stuffed, polar bear rearing up on its hind legs, a pair of very large and thankfully very old elephant tusks, an exquisite *uchikake*—a Japanese wedding over-kimono (worn by a life-size mannequin)—an almost life-size olivewood cross bearing an olivewood Jesus, and thirteen mounted gnu heads. Here and there was the odd piece of furniture; a rare floor model Bavarian cuckoo clock, a nineteenth-century English fainting couch, a maroon Naugahyde armchair, an Italian rococo settee with two matching chairs, and what I can best describe as a throne. The latter was an intricately carved chair, probably Chinese rosewood, that had been gilded to within an inch of its life. And folks think we native Southerners are the eccentric ones.

"May I speak to the captain?" I asked.

"He's not here."

"But you said—"

"Have a seat, Mrs. Timberlake."

"Don't mind if I do," I said, and headed for the throne.

"Not that one. Only the captain sits there."

I sighed and turned toward the nearest rococo chair.

"That's my chair," she snapped.

I took the hint and climbed into the maroon Naugahyde armchair. It smelled of old sweat and cigars. I ordered my stomach to ignore the stench.

"First Mate Keffert," I said, "I really need to speak to your husband."

"I told you the captain is out. You can speak to me."

"Well, okay, but—"

"Not that there's much you can say at this point to redeem yourself."

"*Redeem* myself?"

"Mrs. Timberlake, I'm sure you have no appreciation for the amount of pain your slight has caused us, so allow me to fill you in. It's never easy to move from one part of the country to another, but you folks here in the South have made this move a hellish experience for us."

"How so?" I am nothing but gracious to our immigrant populace from the North.

"Well, for starters, you're all a bunch of phonies."

22

"I beg your pardon!"

"Oh sure, the South is famous for its hospitality, but that's reserved only for visitors. For people who plan to stay, it's quite another thing."

"That's ridiculous."

She was a short woman—even by my standards—with a thick neck and torso, but skinny legs. Seated as she was on the rococo chair, her feet didn't touch the floor. When she shook her head vigorously the spindly appendages swayed back and forth like twin pendulums.

"It's the truth, Mrs. Timberlake. You natives—or perhaps I should say 'y'all'—resent our presence. It's like you're afraid we're taking over or something. Outwardly you're too polite to say anything, but you show it in other ways."

"Like not inviting you to my party? Look—"

"Oh, it's not just that—although I guess that is the straw that broke the camel's back. But take this house, every neighbor within a two-mile radius has seen the inside—taken the grand tour, so to speak—and we've had a number of couples over for dinner, but not a single one has invited us to visit their home."

"Maybe they're intimidated."

"In that case they could invite us out to a restaurant, but the phone never rings."

"Perhaps you have a point, ma'am, but—"

"There's more. I joined a book club—there was an ad for it posted at the library—and has that ever been an eye-opener. Maybe half the women are from the North—the others from the South—but we northern women have learned to keep our mouths shut. All the discussions revolve around the Southern woman's point of view, the Southern cultural experience, the Southern this, the Southern that." She took a deep breath. "Well, let me tell you, Mrs. Timberlake, in my book club back home in Connecticut, we never debated the Yankee point of view. We never even thought to consider it. We just read the damn books and discussed them."

"Well—"

"All this Southern talk isn't limited to the book club, either. There isn't a day that newspaper doesn't have an article about some special aspect of the South. Radio and television do the same thing. It's as if everything has to be interpreted in some sort of special Southern context. Back home we hardly used the word 'North' unless we were giving directions. We certainly weren't obsessed with it."

"That's because you were never an occupied nation," I said quietly. I really didn't intend for her to hear that, but the rich old biddy had the ears of a bat.

"You were a separate nation for four years and that was one hundred and fifty years ago. Get over it!"

I hopped to my feet, too angry to feel pain. "Maybe we resent you because you don't make an effort to understand us. You equate our accents with ignorance and—"

"I'll have you know I do no such thing."

"Well, you certainly interrupt a lot, which is not a Southern trait."

Her face colored. "Point taken. But I've done everything else humanly possibly to fit in. I serve grits for breakfast, we eat hoppin' john at New Year's, and I've even learned to eat okra."

I felt sorry for the woman. She seemed every bit as sincere as Mama's priest does on pledge Sunday.

"It's not purely a food thing, First Mate Keffert. It's well—okay, if you really want to know, I'll tell you."

She nodded vigorously, her legs rising and falling like ripples in the wake of a speedboat.

"It's all about manners," I said, and not without a good deal of guilt. The way I'd been acting lately, I wouldn't be surprised to wake up one morning in King Arthur's Court. "It's about saying yes ma'am, and no sir. It's about biding one's time and waiting patiently in line at the grocery store. It's about—"

"Cutting off drivers in traffic, and tailgating so close you can practically smell the breath of the person behind you?"

"Touché. Look, my mama throws a huge Christmas party every year. I'm sure I can get her to invite you."

"Really?"

"Really. And if I know Mama, she'll be more than happy to give y'all some lessons in Southernness before then. Who knows, by the time the party rolls around, you may even be able to pass."

The first mate beamed. "Thank you, Mrs. Timberlake."

"Please, call me Abby."

"In that case, you may call me Terri. You know what, Abby? I think you and I are going to be friends."

I smiled and stood, careful to put my weight on my left foot. "Terri it is. Say, are you sure your husband's out?"

She looked startled, and then frowned. "Oh yes, he's out. Abby, are you calling me a liar?"

It behooved me to tread carefully. "No, of course not. It's just that—well, heck, Terri, I may as well come right out and say it. I was hoping to get a peek at his armor collection."

She glanced around the room nervously. My eyes followed hers to one of the gnu heads. Was it my imagination, or did I really see a faint glow in one of the beast's glassy eyes? Perhaps the captain was in after all, and spying at me through the mounted head—then again, I've always had an active imagination.

"Abby," she said softly, "I could show you the captain's armor collection, but you'd have to promise never to tell him. Or anyone else for that matter. Things have a way of getting around and Richard—I mean, the captain—would be very upset with me."

"Cross my heart and hope to die, stick a needle in my eye," I said blithely.

She smiled. "Follow me."

I was astounded by all the space inside that stucco ship. Terri led me along passageways lined with tightly closed doors and down flights of stairs so steep, they were virtually nothing more than ladders. Finally, where one would expect to find the engine room on a real ship, she paused outside a low wood door and felt along the lintel for a key.

"Get ready," she said as she unlocked the door. "It's quite something."

I thought I was ready, but nothing could have prepared me for what greeted my eyes when Terri finally found and turned on the light switch. Before me lay a replica of a medieval torture chamber. The walls were made out of concrete stones, of the sort often found in zoo displays. These had been shellacked in areas to make it appear as if they were dripping with moisture. Chains as thick as my wrist hung from the ceiling and extended from the walls, and attached to these by shackles were lifelike figures of people. So real were they that I couldn't help but scream.

Terri laughed. "They're just wax, Abby. Those three are castoffs from Madame Tussaud's Wax Museum in London, and that one came from the

Ripley's museum in Gatlinburg. The rest we acquired from private sales and auctions."

I stared at the morbid exhibits with the fascination of a tourist. The majority of the wax figures were merely shackled to the walls or dangled from the ceiling, but two were hooked up to instruments of torture. One man, his mouth wide open in a silent scream, was stretched across the infamous "rack." A second figure, that of a woman, was about to be embraced by the killing hug of the Iron Maiden.

I caught my breath. "You haven't let your neighbors see this, have you? I mean, if you have, this could be why—"

She laughed again. "Heavens no. This is the private part of our—or should I say, the captain's—private collection. Personally, Abby, I find this creepy."

That was a relief. Not that thirteen gnu heads weren't creepy enough, but I try not to be judgmental. Still, if indeed I did end up in Charleston like Greg wanted, I was going to miss folks like the Kefferts. No doubt Charleston had its share of crazies, too, but it would take me a while to ferret them out.

I glanced around the room again. "I don't see any armor," I said warily. After all, I'd seen that *Twilight Zone* episode in which real people were encased in wax and put on display.

"The armor's through here," she said and pushed lightly against one of the fake stones. At her touch an entire wall, including two chained wax prisoners, swung away from us, revealing a much larger and very different room.

This new chamber contained no obvious horrors. To the contrary, it looked liked a fairy-tale version of a castle throne room. In fact, there were two thrones, one larger than the other, on a dais at the far end, and they made the rosewood throne in the living room look crude by comparison. Resting on each red velvet seat was a gold crown, and over one armrest of the larger throne lay a purple velvet robe with what looked like ermine trim. Leading up to the dais was a runner of red carpet, and on either side stood rows of life-size knights in full armor. These were not wax figures, mind you, but solid wood carvings capable of supporting the weight of their respective regalia.

This time I merely gasped in astonishment. "This is just incredible!"

The room was illuminated by wall-mounted gas torches that had presumably been ignited by the opening of the door. The flickering light was just bright enough for me to see that Terri was blushing.

"Richard and I like to pretend that he's Arthur and that I'm Guinevere. This room is our Camelot."

"Where's the round table?"

She giggled nervously. "That's in another room. Abby, I know you must think we're real nut cases, but we never had children. What I'm trying to say is, this is our hobby. I mean, is it really any different than playing with model trains, or collecting

Raggedy Ann dolls? We're not hurting anyone." She was beginning to sound desperate for approval.

"Except for those poor folks back there," I said with a jerk of my thumb, and laughed.

She smiled gratefully at my joke. "Richard sometimes takes our little game too far. Not that he would ever do that to a real person—I didn't mean that." She shook her head to signify a change of subject. "Well, here's the armor you wanted to see. Of course to us they're knights, and they all have names, but I won't bore you with that."

"Please bore away," I cried. In the dim light I was already examining the nearest suit. Sure enough, it had a neat little dent on the lower right quadrant of the breastplate. However, as I've already made clear, I am no expert on armature. Still, even to my untrained eye this particular suit did not look English. I expressed my observation aloud.

"You're right, it's not," Terri said without batting an eyelash. "This is where Arthur receives visitors from all over the world. These," she said, waving her arms at the rows of knights, "have come to petition admittance to Arthur's court."

She introduced the steel-clad statues as if they were living men, and I, playing along, spoke briefly to each in turn. As I did so, I studied their armature. All but three bore the proof mark, but none was in so fine a shape as the suit in which Tweetie had been found dead. No wonder the

Captain had been so eager to pay big bucks for the mystery armor.

Then a chilling thought crossed my mind; what if Captain Keffert already owned the mystery suit? What if his attempt to purchase the cuirass was merely a ruse?

"Terri," I said calmly, "does the captain—or should I say, the king—ever wear any of the suits?"

She blushed again. "Why would King Arthur dress like a knight?"

"Change can be fun." I've said those same words to Mama innumerable times.

She looked down at the concrete floor. "Sometimes he does like to be Sir Galahad."

"And you? Whom do you like to be?"

"Arthur," she whispered.

"Indeed." I didn't know what else to say.

"Richard enjoys being—well, bossed around. Sometimes if he's really naughty he has to spend time in there." She jerked a thumb in the direction of the torture chamber.

It was my turn to blush. The two of them were probably as old as Mama, for crying out loud. I wasn't about to ask if the Connecticut captain ever played the part of Guinevere.

"Do either of you ever wear the suits out in public? You know, like to Renaissance festivals and such?"

She looked up. The shock on her face was genuine.

"Heavens no. These are valuable pieces. We're

really very careful with them. These rooms are climatically controlled."

"Just asking, dear."

We stood in uncomfortable silence for a moment. "How long has your husband been trying to acquire a genuine seventeenth-century Italian cuirass?" I finally asked.

It was intended as a trick question, but Terri didn't miss a beat. "Ever since he saw it on TV this morning. Frankly, Abby, my husband thinks you've been holding out on him."

"That's ridiculous," I cried. "I told him I don't own that suit."

She put a hand on my arm as if to quiet me and then, much to my surprise, her bony fingers found my wrist and she began to pull me toward the thrones. I tried to slip out of her grasp without seeming rude, but the talons tightened.

"Come with me," she all but purred, "there's a little room behind the dais you've just got to see."

I'd reached my spookiness quota for the day. I gently pried her fingers open with my free hand, and once liberated took a quick step back, almost knocking over a knight.

"I've got an appointment," I said. "Actually, it's a date with a Charlotte detective. I told him to meet me here, because the restaurant we're going to is in Belmont."

Terri glanced at her watch. "It's a little early for dinner, isn't it?"

It's hard to stay on your toes, especially with a

wounded ankle. "He's an *old* detective. He likes his dinner early."

"At three?"

"He goes to bed at seven. Look, I've really got to go."

She stepped forward, her hands outstretched, and that's when I considered bolting. I know it was silly of me. She wasn't that much larger than I and she had a good twenty years on me. If her objective was to turn me into a wax specimen for the Keffert Chamber of Horrors, brute strength was not on her side. Of course, if she'd had a gun in her hand, that would have been another story. But who knew what was literally hiding up her sleeve? Or, for all I knew, the floor beneath me could suddenly give way and I'd plunge into a pit replete with pendulum.

If it is better to be safe than sorry, then it is better to be a fool than to risk being turned into a giant candle. So bolt is what I did. I fled through the torture room and down the long hallway. My adrenaline was pumping so hard I didn't even feel my foot. As for the steep metal stairs, I think I must have flown up them.

At last I stumbled, panting, into the warm autumn sunshine. A mockingbird singing in the crape myrtle and the distant drone of boats on the lake assured me that all was right with the world

"You silly fool," I muttered to myself. Then, just as quickly as I could, I got in my car and drove off to tilt at another windmill.

23

The traffic gods were with me and it took me only a half hour to get to Myers Park. I'd driven by the Larkins' house a number of times, but had never had the occasion to stop in. It was time to invent one.

"Hey there," I said, oozing mock cheer, when Regina opened the door. "You didn't, by any chance, happen to leave this behind last night?" I held up a small blue umbrella folded to the size of a large sausage. It was a near permanent resident under the front seat of my car.

Regina is about my age, but she has it together in a way I'll never have. In honor of the season she was dressed in a camel skirt, topped by a rust cashmere sweater. She was wearing pantyhose—something I try to avoid as much as possible—and her camel and rust shoes, by Gucci, I think, undoubtedly cost more than my monthly car payment. A simple gold wrist bangle and gold hoop earrings completed the look of casual elegance.

It wouldn't have been so bad if Regina had been a homely woman. But she was, as my son Charlie would describe a woman his own age, "a real babe." A few wisps of gray aside, the woman couldn't have aged much since high school. I look young for my age as well, but undeniably there are parts of me that have migrated southward. Regina, on the other hand, was disgustingly in place. I would have been intensely jealous were it not for the knowledge that often people who appear to have it all together on the outside are suffering deeply on the inside. I don't have any proof that this is so, and I can't even remember where I read that, but I choose to believe it is true.

She stared at the compact umbrella I waved before her, looking utterly confused. I wasn't sure she'd heard my question.

"Is this yours?" I asked again.

Regina shook her head. "Gracious no," she drawled, without a trace of Yankee accent. "It didn't rain last night."

I smiled pleasantly. She was going to be a hard nut to crack. Both Regina and her husband, Donald, are chameleons. If I hadn't heard from a reliable source—Wynnell knows her Yankees every bit as well as she knows her armor—I never would have guessed that the couple originally hailed from Poughkeepsie, New York. Over the twenty-odd years they've lived in Charlotte they've shed every trace of Northern beginnings and become virtual Southerners.

Don't get me wrong. There is nothing wrong with trying to fit in, as long as one's motives are pure. After all, imitation is the highest form of flattery. The Larkins, however, had done an uncanny job of melding with the locals, so uncanny in fact, that in my book they were suspect. If you ask me, anyone capable of such total assimilation is capable of just about anything. Lying was a given. As for murder—well, I'd just have to see about that.

"But thanks for checking," Regina said as she started to close the door.

I waved the umbrella again. "Well, I just wanted to make sure this wasn't yours."

Like I said, Regina, when not yelling at me for having been evicted from my party, was practically the genuine thing. She paused and pretended to think things over.

"Well, silly me," she said, as if she'd suddenly seen the light. "I don't know where I left my manners. Won't you come in, Mrs. Timberlake?"

"Well, uh—" I said just to be polite.

Regina stepped aside, a broad hostess grin on her face. "I've just made a fresh pitcher of sweet tea. The chocolate chip cookies I made this morning."

"Don't mind if I do," I said, with perhaps just a tad too much gusto. Even if Regina proved to be no more informative than the local five o'clock news, the tea and cookies would certainly hit the spot. After what might have happened at the Kefferts' house, a sugar fix was definitely in order.

I took two steps into the large foyer and stopped dead in my tracks. Ahead of me was a doorway that opened onto a wide hall, but on either side stood a full suit of armor. I must have gasped.

"Sort of takes one aback, doesn't?" Regina said with a laugh. "Personally, I think it's too much. I'm trying to get Donald to donate them to a museum somewhere. Maybe the Mint."

I scrutinized the suit on my left. There were a number of small round holes on the breastplate, but no dents. The entire garniture was beautifully etched in an intricate design.

"Are they real?"

Regina laughed generously, her mouth opening to an astonishing size. "Oh yes. We picked them up on a trip to Heidelberg a couple of years ago. According to the dealer, the one you're looking at may have—or I should say, some of the pieces may have—belonged to Emperor Maximilian I. Well, when he was Archduke Maximilian of Austria, at any rate."

"But I don't see a proof mark," I wailed. Sometimes my mouth deserves a good shushing.

Regina laughed again. "That's because these pieces were made in the mid-fifteen hundreds. Firearms were not such an issue then."

I cringed. Oh, the shame of knowing less about an antiquity than one of my regular clients.

"Do you have others besides these two?"

"No, just these two. Mrs. Timberlake, I didn't realize you were so interested in armor." Her lips arranged themselves into a smile, but I know an accusation when I hear one. Regina Larkin was telling me loud and clear that she fully suspected my visit was in connection with Tweetie's death.

The best way to allay any suspicions was to

come clean—well, not squeaky clean, of course. "I've never had a keen interest in it," I said. "At least not until last night. I guess you know by now that my ex-husband's wife was found dead in a suit of armor."

"In your house, I believe."

I must confess that I'd driven all the way to Myers Park with only loosely formulated questions in my mind. I needed a few more minutes to focus.

"That's correct," I said calmly. "Say, didn't you say something about sweet tea and cookies?"

"That I did! Mercy me, where are my manners? Please, Mrs. Timberlake, follow me."

I noted with satisfaction that Regina called me Mrs. Timberlake, and not Abby. That was very Southern of her. Until I gave her permission to use my first name, she could not presume a personal relationship. Her invitation to my party, mind you, had been purely a business consideration.

She led me into what was quite obviously the formal living room. That was fine with me. Some folks feel more welcome when invited into the den, but I had no desire to cozy up with Pinocchio. Not after her accusations the night before. I may be a lot smaller than an elephant, but my memory is just as long.

Regina excused herself to the kitchen, and I took advantage of her absence to study the room. It was far more traditional and understated than the pair of metal warriors in the hall might suggest. The color scheme was drawn from a large, predominantly yellow and rose Aubusson rug of floral design, which was centered on the highly polished hardwood floor. The walls were papered in the same pale yellow, and the drapes were just a few shades darker. There were two couches flanking the fireplace at right angles, and their background was rose. Here and there were small touches of green, also drawn from the rug. Two cream and rose Chinese prints, in black lacquered frames, hung on either side of the mantel. They were the only exotic touches.

I sighed deeply. It was such a disappointment to find so little to criticize. I'd been selling to the Larkins for years, and recognized the rug as one of my former wares. Still, it would have given me great satisfaction to learn that they had been secretly buying kitsch, worthy of the Kefferts, from other dealers.

"Here you are," Regina said, interrupting my reverie. She was carrying a sterling tray, upon which she'd arranged a plate of cookies, two cloth napkins, and a pair of very tall glasses filled almost to the brim with tea. Her movements were graceful and the tea was in no danger of slopping over the edges—not until a glass found its way into my hands.

I decided to postpone my fate by starting with a chocolate chip cookie. Just for the record, they were the soft variety, and so good I had my doubts they were homemade. Even good cooks like Mama tend to overbrown the edges.

"So," I said, willing myself not to make smacking noises, "from what I can see, your armor is not in a climate-controlled environment. Isn't that important?"

Regina took a leisurely sip of her sweet tea. I regret to report she didn't spill a drop.

"The house is air-conditioned in the summer and heated in the winter. That's certainly what I would call climate-controlled."

I reached for my tea with studied casualness. Before the glass cleared the tray I managed to spill a good tablespoon full. I mopped the silver tray with my napkin. At least the cookies were still dry.

"But you keep them in the foyer," I said stupidly. "Isn't the humidity a problem?"

"Heavens no. In Europe you'll find armor in the dankest castles you can imagine. Of course you wouldn't want to get the pieces wet, if you can help it, but it's not like we wash them."

"Do you ever take them outside?"

She took another sip of tea. "Oh, I get it now. You think there's a possibility one of us wore a suit of armor to your party. Is that it?"

"I said no such thing." If I was that transparent, just like the Invisible Man, I was going to have to pay closer attention to what I ate.

"Because that wouldn't make any sense, would it? Donald came as Geppetto, and I came as Pinocchio. You spoke to us both, don't you remember? Or have you forgotten that terrible scene in which you threw us all out on our ears?"

I shook my head. No doubt I'd go to my grave with that mark against me. I could see the epitaph carved on my tombstone now. "Here lies Abigail Louise Wiggins Timberlake, who threw a hissy fit, and in the process tossed Charlotte's crème de la crème out on their collective ears."

Oh well, at least I'd be immortalized. "Don't do what Abigail Timberlake did," generations of Carolina women would whisper to their daughters as they prepared for Cotillion. And if any of these young women heeded that sage advice, my death would not have been in vain.

Regina had the grace not to smile openly at my discomfort. Instead she smirked behind the rim of her tea glass, her chin protruding just below the bottom.

"Besides, Mrs. Timberlake, that wasn't a German suit we saw at your party last night."

I nodded. "It was Italian. Mrs. Larkin, I don't think you or your husband dressed up in that suit, but—well, is it possible you loaned it to a friend?"

Even a Southern lady—and Regina was only a pseudo-Southern lady—can be pushed only so far. With a trembling hand she put down her glass and then stood.

"Mrs. Timberlake, you've said quite enough. As I've already told you, the German armatures in the foyer are the only two we own. But even if that were not the case, why would we, or any of our friends, wish to kill the second Mrs. Timberlake? If you ask me, you, more than anyone, had a motive."

I'm a fairly good actress, and indignation has always been my forte. I jumped to my feet, let out a loud cry of pain, and sank back on the pale rose couch. I think my guardian angels must have been on red alert, because not a single drop more of tea spilled from my glass.

Regina smiled in relief. "Look, Mrs. Timberlake, perhaps that was unfair of me. I can understand how desperate you must be to have the killer apprehended, but you're barking up the wrong tree. There were folks with motives there last night—besides you, I mean. However, my husband and I did not number among them."

Boy, did that get my attention. "Who?" I cried.

She picked up a cookie and pretended to nibble, but she wasn't fooling me. It wouldn't have surprised me if *her* tea was unsweetened.

If I'd had longer arms, I might have been tempted to slap the cookie out of her hand. "*Who* had a motive to kill Tweetie? And please don't say Wynnell Crawford."

Her eyes widened. "Why on earth would I say that?"

"No reason. Whom did you mean?"

"Well," she finally said, "there's that Lynne Meredith."

"The mermaid? But that wouldn't have been possible. Even if Lynne had brought the suit of armor with her and kept it in the car, hoping to stuff Tweetie's body in it, she couldn't have done it. She had a tail, for crying out loud. She couldn't even walk."

"Ah, but Neptune could, right?"

"His name is Roderick. And I suppose he could,

but—say, you didn't see him leave the room for any length of time, did you?"

She shrugged and put the cookie down. "There were a lot of people. I suppose he could have set that Meredith woman on a chair, or couch, and excused himself for a few minutes. *Or*"—she leaned forward conspiratorially—"the mermaid could have hired a hit man."

"But why? What would her motive be?"

"Mrs. Timberlake, haven't you heard?"

I smiled smugly. "Of course, but it's just a rumor. Roderick was Tweetie's tennis instructor—for a little while at least—but he never slept with her."

"Oh, but he did."

"Says who?"

Regina's eyes burned brightly with the joy that comes only by imparting a juicy morsel of gossip. "That Meredith woman told me herself."

"Get out of town! Why, just today at lunch the two of them told me that was just a rumor."

"She said that as well?"

I nodded. "But I guess I should have known better, because he was copping a feel that very moment."

Regina frowned. She was either too highborn to know the expression, or was feigning ignorance.

"He was groping me," I explained. "Right in front of Lynne—well, maybe not right in front, but behind the table."

"That's disgusting."

"Tell me about it. I stabbed him with my fork."

"You didn't!"

I hung my head. "Yes, I did."

"You go, girl!"

"What?" I looked up at a brand-new Regina. Gone was the pseudo-Southern Stepford wife. In her place was a red-blooded, all-American girl. Not that we Southerners don't have red blood as well, but you know what I mean.

"Abby—do you mind if I call you that?"

"Not if I may call you Regina."

"Please do. Anyway, the same thing happened to me."

"You stabbed the boy toy?"

"No, but I wish I had. We were having lunch at the club—say, you don't belong, do you?"

I shook my head. There was no point even in asking which club. I know she didn't mean the American Automobile Association, which, outside of my book club, the Blue Stockings, is the only nonprofessional organization to which I do belong.

"Well anyway, as I was saying, Donald and I were having lunch, when this Meredith woman with her—what did you call him?"

"Boy toy."

"Yes! She'd been having a tennis lesson and they were still dressed in their whites. She claimed to have met me at some fund-raiser last spring. Of course I didn't know who she was from Adam, although the young man looked vaguely familiar. I'd probably seen him out on the courts. At any rate, we didn't even invite them to sit, but they did anyway. Can you imagine that?"

"How rude," I said sympathetically.

"Oh, but that was only the beginning. She said she liked the looks of my shrimp salad, and before I could do anything to stop her, she'd picked up my dessert fork and taken a bite."

I gasped. Surely that was rude in all fifty states.

"Did you say anything?"

"I suggested she might like to order one of her own, and do you know what she said? She said it hadn't tasted all that good, so she ordered chicken instead. But that didn't stop her from taking two more bites!"

"With her used fork?"

"Yes." Regina closed her eyes at the painful memory. "So you see, Abby, I was already distracted when I felt something rubbing against my leg under the table. At first I thought it was a cat or something, and was trying to figure out how one had gotten into the club, and then—well, it soon became very clear this wasn't a cat."

"What did you do?"

"I told Donald I was feeling sick—which I was by then—and we came right home."

I wanted to ask her just exactly *what* it was that Roderick was rubbing against her, but although we were now on a first-name basis, we weren't that close. In the end I decided it had to be one of his feet. Either that or my ex-husband Buford was not the poster boy for American manhood that he claimed to be.

"So when did Lynne Meredith tell you Roderick was cheating on her?"

"That very night. She called to say there was something she just had to tell me, and could she please come over. I told her we had plans for the evening, that we were going out, but she wouldn't take no for an answer. She asked if she could tell her problem over the phone. I said no as politely as I could, but it was like she hadn't even heard me. She plunged right in and told me the whole sordid tale."

I could feel my mouth salivating in anticipation of the juicy details. "And?"

24

"Well, it seems *that* woman received an anonymous call from a female telling her where and when she could find the tennis instructor in bed with another woman. So that woman—"

"You mean Lynne Meredith, right?"

Regina showed her good breeding by restricting her eye rolling to a quarter of a turn. "That's correct. Anyway, as I was about to say, that woman raced over to her lover's house—they don't live together, you know—and found him in flagrante delicto with Tweetie Timberlake. There were, of course, words exchanged, in which the woman recognized the voice of the second Mrs. Timberlake."

I gasped. Why on earth would Tweetie set herself up for exposure, no pun intended? Unless— that was it! To get back at Buford! Tweetie had been sleeping her way around town to punish one of the most powerful men in Charlotte. Had I not had two children to consider when Buford stepped out on me, I might have done the same thing. I wouldn't have slept with Ed Crawford, of course, but I might have had a good time playing with the boy toy. *Might* have. I'd like to think my morals exert a stronger pull than my hormones. It's just that I know I'm not perfect.

"Did you ever met the second Mrs. Timberlake?" I asked.

Regina shook her well-coiffed head. "No, but I'd seen her picture on the society page a number of times. I knew exactly who that horrible woman was talking about. At any rate, Ms. Meredith asked what I would do if I were in her place. Can you believe that? As if I would ever cheat on my Donald."

I murmured sympathetic noises of disbelief and outrage.

"Perhaps it was unkind of me, Abby, but at that point I just hung up the phone."

"You did?" My heart sank. No juicy tidbits were ever garnered from a phone in its cradle.

"I certainly did. Forgive me for saying this, Abby, but I was horrified to see that woman and her boy thing show up at your party last night."

"That's boy *toy*," I said kindly.

Regina waited for me to continue, perhaps even to apologize. Either way she was out of luck. I had people to see, and miles to drive, before I slept. But my visit to Regina had been far more productive that I'd dared hope. I'm no psychologist, but if you ask me, the two biggest motives for murder are greed and revenge. I saw both of those at play here. Roderick would have been very angry at Tweetie for potentially sabotaging the arrangement he had with Lynne Meredith, and hence the revenge aspect. As for the greed, well—Lynne was the goose that laid the golden eggs, and as such, a far more valuable bird than Tweetie.

I stood. "You've been very gracious, Regina. The tea and cookies were absolutely delicious."

"I'm glad you liked them," my impromptu hostess said somewhat stiffly. I could tell she was still miffed because I'd corrected her.

We headed for the door, just as the bell rang. Instinctively I hung back.

"Go ahead and answer it," I urged. "I'll wait right here. I just remembered there is something rather important I forgot to say."

Poor Regina looked like a couch potato who'd been asked to choose between the remote and a bag of chips. She did a little two-step that got her nowhere, but when the bell rang again, the die was cast. I retreated further into the living room while she practically sprinted to the door.

"Oh," I heard her say. "I didn't expect you this early."

"I would have called, but I lost your number." This speaker was male and sounded vaguely familiar. "And," he added, an edge of accusation to his voice, "you're not listed.

"Well this is rather an awkward time, you see, because I have company."

There was either a long pause, or the parties at the door were whispering. Unable to contain my curiosity, I crept in their direction. I would have tiptoed but my sprained ankle prevented that.

"Do you still want it?" he asked.

I froze.

"Yes, of course I still want it. At first I thought it was too big, that it wouldn't fit."

"Did you measure your space?"

"This morning. It will fit fine. But like I said I have a visitor."

The man at the door mumbled something that I couldn't follow, but I very clearly heard Regina say my name. Throwing caution to the wind I stepped boldly in their direction, and in so doing placed my foot in such a way that a lightning bolt of pain shot up as high as my armpit. My howl of pain was short-lived, because I hit the floor like a chicken on a June bug. For a moment I didn't even know what had happened to me.

The next voice I remember hearing was Regina's. "I'm sure she'll be all right," she was saying, as she slid an ottoman under my injured extremity. I was lying at a forty-five degree angle across one of the rose couches.

"Well, well, well," the man said, shaking his head. He towered over me, his face in the shadow, but I recognized now the voice of Moses, AKA Allan Bills, the antique dealer from Charleston, South Carolina.

"A well is a deep hole in the ground," I said.

"That joke wasn't funny even in the fourth grade, Abby. Surely you can do better than that."

I glared up at the giant. "I thought you went back to Charleston."

"Not without transacting a little business first.

Otherwise this trip would have been a total waste."

"I don't see how you can say that. Didn't you have fun dumping that bowl of punch on my Berber?"

He chuckled. "That was mildly amusing, yes."

"And I'm sure you plan to tell everyone you know in Charleston about that fiasco of a party."

"Of course."

I struggled to my good foot. "Then your trip was worth every penny you spent on it. You don't need to be undercutting my business by selling to my customers up here."

"Abby," Regina said with surprising sharpness, "who I buy from is really not your business."

She was right, of course. But Alan Bills had the entire low country of South Carolina at his disposal. He didn't need to peddle his wares up in Charlotte. In fact, it just didn't make sense. There were too many fine shops in the area. Whatever it was he had, I was sure Regina Larkin could find locally. That didn't stop me from being irritated.

"For your information, Mr. Smarty Pants," I said, reverting to the fourth grade Abby, "I'm moving to Charleston, and I plan to open a shop there. How will you like it if I poach some of your customers?"

Alan Bills, who was dressed in blue jeans and a long-sleeved navy polo shirt, didn't look anything like Moses by the light of day. His sneer, however, was worthy of pharaoh.

"*You* opening a shop in Charleston? Boy, that's a laugh."

"I don't have to stand here and be insulted," I humphed, and limped to the door.

Regina suddenly remembered her Southern manners and flew to open it. "Abby," she said softly, laying a well-manicured hand on my shoulder, "what I said about that Meredith woman and her, uh, plaything—"

"You mean boy toy, don't you?"

"Yes, well, you won't repeat that, will you?"

"Don't be silly, dear."

That wasn't good enough for Regina. "Abby, do you promise?"

I tried to slip past her. I am not a habitual gossip, mind you, but this tidbit might come in handy in assuaging Mama, assuming she wasn't wild about my forsaking the house next door and moving to Charleston. Besides, you never know when a promise made in good faith will suddenly turn on you, biting you on the behind.

Regina grabbed my left arm. "Abby, promise!"

I crossed the fingers on my right hand. "Okay, I promise."

The talons released me, and she arranged her lips into a smile that would make a Junior Leaguer proud. "Y'all come back now, hear?"

"Y'all is a plural term," I said meanly. "You should know that by now."

I stumbled to my car, thoroughly ashamed of myself, and not a little bit pleased.

*   *   *

I drove less than a block before pulling over into the shade of a massive laurel oak that was just beginning to lose its leaves. It was time to think, time to lay out a strategy. Exercising my gray cells gets increasingly difficult with the passing years, and I now had to contend with the distraction of a throbbing ankle. Not to mention—at the risk of being crude—that Bubba's Chinese buffet was seeking a quick exit.

As I saw it, there were two more visits to be made before I could dine with Greg. But in which order? Although it would probably get me nowhere but deeper in trouble, I felt a need to return to the scene of the crime. Not *my* crime, but that of whoever killed the Widow Saunders. Perhaps there were clues to be gleaned from her secretary, pretty-boy Caleb. Clues that would exonerate me of any suspicion. I wasn't really worried that I would be charged in the old woman's death—I didn't have a motive as far as I could see—but it would be nice to get that bullying Barb off my back.

The second item on my agenda was far more important. I did have a motive to kill Tweetie—albeit a rather stale motive. Revenge is a dish best served cold, Shakespeare said, but this was ridiculous. No one could eat from a dish more than four years old, no matter how well it had been chilled. Still, the woman had been found dead in my house, under my bed. It behooved me to come up with a suspect other than myself or my best friend Wynnell, for that matter. If indeed Lynne Meredith's tennis instructor did the dastardly deed, I stood as good a chance as the police of getting him to confess.

I fumbled around in my glove box, found the cassette recorder I take with me to flea markets to help me keep track of bargains, and tucked the tiny machine between my breasts. It was a tight fit. Magdalena Yoder, a friend of mine up in Pennsylvania, has a sister who totes a minuscule mutt around in her bra. In fact, Magdalena sometimes carries a kitten around in hers. Of course, neither of those ladies is as blessed in the mammary department as yours truly. I had to loosen my straps and set the back hooks on the most generous setting, and even then a wrong move might accidentally activate the contraption.

Please believe me when I tell you that I'm not a total fool. Before heading for the Meredith estate I checked my pepper spray. It worked fine. I would have called Greg, or Mama, to tell them of my destination, except that I don't own a cell phone, and Myers Park is not exactly spilling over with public booths. I know, I should get with it and purchase one of the little contraptions, but until they prove conclusively they don't cause brain tumors, and until I can master the art of putting on mascara on the move, my petite palms shall remain phoneless while I'm not at home. I'm just not that coordinated.

Fortunately, both the Meredith and Saunders homes are within a five-mile drive from the Larkin house, just in opposite directions. Without my bum ankle I might even have attempted to walk to Lynne's. I drove, however, and using the caution I pride myself on having, I made sure her neighbors knew I was there. After the third honk, even Lynne got the idea.

"Abby," she called from her open front door, "what the hell are you doing?"

You see what I mean about Lynne Meredith being from up the road a piece? I stuck my head out the window and hollered back.

"I didn't mean to do it! My seat belt was stuck, and while I was trying to undo it, I sort of bumped the horn. I'll be right there!"

She started to come toward me, but I slid out onto my good foot and slammed the door behind me. The retort was almost loud enough to set off her neighbors' alarms.

Lynne held the door open for me, frowning, as I hobbled up her flagstone walk. Just as I reached the steps, Roderick appeared over her shoulder. His eyes were lit up like a jack-o'-lantern with *three* candles. If the poor misguided soul was anticipating a ménage à trois, he was out of luck. The temptation to rub one's hands over a man's abs is no indicator of promiscuity. Greg is, and will always be, the only man for me.

"Hey y'all," I said brightly, but loud enough for neighbors to hear two doors down, "mind if I come in?" I suppose a really wise Abby would have planned to conduct the interview on the front porch, but I suspected the brazen Buckeyes were more likely to spill their guts in the privacy of Lynne's sumptuously appointed home.

"Sure, come on," Roderick said.

Lynne's furrowed brows were in need of more cotton seed. "We were just about to go out."

"No, we weren't." Roderick was even denser than I.

"Come in then," Lynne snapped. "But the place is a mess and I don't have a thing on hand to serve you."

Even a pseudo-Southern woman always has *something* to serve, if only just a glass of milk past its expiration date. Nevertheless, I was happy to be given entrée. I'd been to the house on several occasions to supervise the placement of pieces purchased from my shop. In all fairness, Lynne has impeccable taste. Her preference is for French Provincial, although she has couple of English Regency pieces tucked in conspicuous places. If her definition of a "mess" is an open magazine on the coffee table and a box of facial tissues in their original cardboard container, then I am doomed to spend eternity wandering through a maze of teenagers' bedrooms.

"Have a seat," Lynne directed.

"Mind if I use the bathroom first?"

Lynne shrugged. "But it's an even bigger mess."

I took my chances. The *Reader's Digest* on the tank lid had a bent cover, and the bottom edge of one of the hand towels was not quite parallel to the floor. I masked my gasp with a flush.

When I returned I chose an armchair that had its

own footstool. My ankle was beginning to feel like Wile E. Coyote at the end of a Road Runner cartoon. If my foot took a notion to just fall off before the end of the day, I would not be surprised.

Lynne and Roderick sat on a settee facing me, across the "messy" coffee table. Lynne wore an expression of annoyed wariness, Roderick's face radiated pure lust.

"So," she said, "to what do we owe the honor of your visit?"

I jabbed at the on button between my bosoms. It took four tries to get the darn thing to start recording. I'm sure the couple opposite thought I was either nuts, or coming on to them.

"I came to talk about sex, dear," I finally said.

25

Try that as your opening line sometime. It is a sure way to get folks' attention.

"Say what?"

"Those rumors you warned me about at lunch today at Bubba's, they're true, aren't they?"

"Why I never!" Lynne practically bellowed. "That's the most offensive thing I've ever heard."

"What's offensive is for Lothario there to play footsies with a married woman in front of her husband. You should be ashamed, Roderick."

He merely winked at my admonition.

Lynne stood angrily. "Who told you this? Who have you been talking to?"

I wasn't going to reveal my source unless I absolutely had to. "You can't deny this, Lynne. And you can't deny that your juvenile joy machine jumped in the sack with Tweetie Timberlake. You caught them yourself."

She sat heavily. "It was Regina Larkin, wasn't it?"

I pleaded the Fifth.

"Why, that little bitch! Thinks she's so high and

mighty just because she's lived here longer than I.
Just you wait—" She caught herself. "That was girl
talk shared in confidence. It's really none of your
business."

I shrugged before turning my gaze to Roderick.
He squirmed like a worm on a fishhook.

"Wherever did you find such an exquisite
cuirass?" I asked.

I might as well have asked him to recite a pas-
sage from a poem he'd learned during his recent
experience in high school. Any poem that didn't
have the word "Nantucket" in it.

"The armor," I said patiently. "The one you
stuffed Tweetie into."

An enormous vein popped out on Roderick's
broad forehead. Between it and Lynne's furrows,
the two shared a smooth complexion.

"What the hell are you talking about, Mrs. Timberlake?" Lynne felt free to call me Abby, but Roderick knew he was too young.

"What I want to know is," I said calmly, "didn't
you feel at all foolish leaving my party as Little Bo
Peep?"

Roderick leaped to his feet. "Lynne, make this
woman leave."

I pointed a warning finger at the middle-aged
Mata Hari. "I'd stay out of this if I were you. He's
the one who killed Tweetie and who's going to be
spending his life behind bars. You are an accessory
after the fact, but I know folks in the department,
and I'm sure I could talk them into going easy on
you. What you still see in this roaming Romeo is

beyond me. I'd have dumped him the second I found him trysting with Big Bird's sister."

Lynne's mouth opened wide enough to catch a sparrow. Fortunately there were none loose in the house. For a moment I thought I'd hit paydirt.

"I have to admit," I said, "that was a quick switcheroo your stud muffin pulled off. Frankly, I don't know how he did it. I mean, I saw Neptune here arrive carrying you, and at some point I remember seeing the knight in shining armor. Y'all must have had the armor hidden someplace handy. Where was it, in the trunk of your car?"

By then Lynne had managed to regain control of her lower jaw. "You're nuts," she hissed. "You're as crazy as the Mad Hatter. If you don't leave right now, I'm calling the police."

"Call away," I said merrily. I squinted, pretending to give her the once-over. "I think you'll look good in stripes. But ask for vertical, if they give you a choice. With those hips of yours—"

"Roderick!" she screamed.

Loverboy stood. He seemed eager to put his hands on me, if only to give me the old heave-ho.

"Touch me," I warned, "and I'll sue the pants off you."

That brought a grin to Lothario's lips. "Anything you say, babe."

I fumbled in my purse, but managed to find the pepper spray before he could reach me. "Back off!" I barked.

The grin broadened. "I've always liked a

woman with fire. How about you and I making some sweet music together?"

"Roderick!" Lynne's face was contorted with rage.

He looked first at her, and then at me. She had the bucks, and I had the body, petite as it might be. I'm not bragging, mind you, but that seemed to be what was going on in that undeveloped mind.

Apparently Lynne can read a blank mind as well as I. She wagged a finger with a long, pink nail. At him, not at me.

"This is the last straw," she hissed. "I put up with those twins in Ohio because I thought you might be trainable. I put up with Tweetie and Regina and—"

"Regina?" I asked, flabbergasted. "Regina Larkin?"

Lynne's thick torso twisted in my direction. "That woman is not the Southern lady you think she is."

"Well, I know she wasn't born here but—"

"Abby, you're not a very good judge of character, are you?"

I glanced at Romeo. "At least I don't cavort with murderers."

The lust left his eyes. "I didn't kill Tweetie, you little bitch."

Despite what Lynne had just said, I am a good judge of character. I know someone capable of murder is quite capable of lying, but there was something about Roderick's voice that made me believe him. He sounded just like my son Charlie had when I falsely accused him of backing my car through the closed garage door. Little did I know at the time that the damage was caused by his sister, Susan, who had sneaked out to go drinking.

At any rate, I backed toward the door. "Well, y'all, this has been a very entertaining visit. We'll have to do this again sometime."

They simultaneously uttered a two-word phrase, the first word of which I, being a true Southern lady, will not repeat. Suffice it to say, it is an anatomical impossibility.

"Your hand towel in the powder room is crooked," I said, and then turned tail and ran.

On the short drive to the late Widow Saunders's mansion, I had a chance to revamp my strategy. Life was not like *Matlock*. You couldn't get someone to confess simply by confronting them with their guilt. At least if they weren't guilty. No, you either had to catch them in the act—with a videotape in hand—or find some other form of hard evidence that would hold up in court.

Unfortunately I didn't even have any real suspects in the widow's death. It could have been Caleb, but unless he was in her will, in a major way, he had nothing to gain. As I saw it, the young man had stood a far better chance of profiting by accompanying the wealthy woman to Genoa.

Perhaps it was the chauffeur. The widow had said nothing about taking the staff with her. But was the loss of one's job sufficient motive to kill? If it was, how many employees did the old bag have?

So there you have it. I had no suspects and didn't know what I was looking for. All I knew was that I had to find or think of something that proved I didn't do the widow in. I know, it was more likely that Congress would abolish the current tax code and replace it with something intelligible than I would find what I needed. But sometimes a gal just has to do what a gal has to do. I realize now that is a lame excuse, and probably the same one Tweetie used the first time she jumped Buford's bones—or he hers—but that's how it was.

I parked in the same spot I had the previous time. It was as an innocuous a place as any. This time, however, I wasn't going to charge up to the front door. Or should I? Perhaps the best thing I could do for myself would be to calmly walk up to the officer on duty—surely there was still someone guarding the crime scene from the likes of me— and strike up a casual conversation.

Better yet, I could come right out and announce my intentions. "Hey, I'm Abigail Louise Timberlake and I'm here to prove that I didn't do the old lady in. I'm not even an official suspect, mind you, but I have too much on my plate right now to even be on anyone's list of suspects. Especially if that anyone happens to be a tall, leggy, man-eating blond named Barb."

My reverie was interrupted by someone across the street calling, "Mama!"

I ignored the caller. He was a man, and obviously not calling to me. Funny though, but when the kids were young, and I was in a public place, every time I heard that four letter word, I practically got whiplash. I knew the sound of my children, of course, but I was conditioned. Every mother is. Every father, too.

"Mama!" The voice was closer.

I glanced around and was startled to see my son Charlie headed my way. He's a full-time student at Winthrop University in Rock Hill, and seldom gets up to Charlotte now that he's developed a circle of friends down there.

"Charlie!"

He loped across the street in my direction. Loping is something I will never have the privilege of doing. But Charlie inherited Buford's height, along with Buford's lighter coloring and regular features. Fortunately, he doesn't seem to have inherited any of his father's reptilian tendencies.

"Mama," he said, not even panting, "I've been expecting you."

"What? But that's impossible. Nobody knows where I am."

He gave me a quick kiss on the cheek. "Get real, Mama. Greg knows where you are. Susan knows where you are. Maybe we don't know exactly where you are at all times, but we know you're trying to clear yourself of any suspicion in Tweetie's death. In that old lady's, too."

"That 'old lady' was Mrs. Saunders," I said. "Or Widow Saunders, if you prefer."

"Yeah, well you don't need to worry about her anymore."

"Charlie, dear, don't speak ill of the dead."

"I'm not, Mama. But Caleb just confessed."

"He did?"

"Yeah. I was here when he did it. Man, it was something."

"Charlie, I think I'm missing a few pieces. Do you know Caleb?"

"Mama, can we talk about this someplace else?"

I looked at my son. Besides looking stressed, he looked thinner than I'd remembered.

"When's the last time you ate?" I asked.

"Mama, you know I hate dorm food."

"You don't hate McDonald's, dear, and there is one just across Cherry Road from the campus."

"Yeah, well, I'm not into food right now. Anyway, can't we go someplace else to talk about this?"

It was a bit of a drive, but I had him follow me down to Carolina Place Mall. After all, he looked like he could use a pair of new jeans as well. Maybe even some shoes.

If indeed my son wasn't into food, you sure couldn't tell it by the way he tucked into the pizza he ordered in the food court. I, of course, had to save my appetite for dinner with Greg, but I nibbled slowly on the smallest slice between sips of sweet tea.

"Okay," I said, "tell me everything, starting with how you know Caleb."

Charlie, who had made me wait until his order

was ready before divulging what he knew, swallowed a bite big enough to feed a small Third World country. He burped loudly before remembering where he was, and with whom.

"Sorry about that, Mama. Anyway, I know Caleb because he has a younger brother, Josh, who's in my chemistry class. The old lady—I mean, Mrs. Saunders—has a pool table. A swimming pool, too. So, once when she was out someplace, Caleb had us over to mess around." Charlie grabbed my hand. "Don't worry, Mama, we didn't do anything stupid like smoke pot or anything—not that I would anyway—or touch her stuff. Like I said, we were just hanging out.

"Anyhow, this afternoon I was just sitting there in my room studying—I've got this big history test tomorrow, and kind of got behind on account of spending too much time thinking about Halloween—when the phone rings and it's Josh telling me his brother was arrested, and could my dad be his lawyer. I told him Daddy wasn't that kind of lawyer, and wasn't even in the country." He paused. "Is he?"

"He's on his way back. He should be home late tonight."

"Yeah, that's what I thought."

"Caleb," I nearly screamed. "Please, dear, get to the part about Caleb killing Widow Saunders."

Charlie's young face screwed up in obvious bewilderment. "Man, I didn't even understand what Caleb saw in that old—I mean, Mrs. Saunders—I sure the hell don't understand why he killed her.

Josh said it had something to do with her going off to Europe, and Caleb not wanting to go. He was afraid she'd dump him for some Italian man and the gig would be over. Something like that. Josh thinks his brother got Mrs. Saunders to write him in her will. Do you think Daddy could find out if that's true?"

I shrugged and took a much-needed sip of sweet tea.

Charlie sighed. "Yeah, well I guess it doesn't make a difference, does it? I mean, they won't let him keep it. Not that he should anyway. Man, especially not after what he did to you."

I sprayed tea over what was left of Charlie's pizza. "*Me?* What did he do to me?"

Charlie hung his head. "Shit, I should have my big mouth sewn shut."

"Too late, dear." It was my turn to grab a wrist. "You can't stop now."

He didn't even try to pull away. "Sorry, Mama. I mean about the swearing and all."

"Forget that," I said. "Spill!"

"Well, it was like this. According to Josh, his brother was waiting for just the right moment to do the widow in, and then you came long. What with Wynnell finding a dead woman in your house, Caleb figured the police would jump to conclusions and suspect you."

"My, that is jumping to conclusions," I said, my temper flaring. "I didn't have the slightest motive. Hell, I'd never even met the old bag before."

Charlie laughed. "Take it easy, Mama. I know

that. Anybody sane would know that. Except for
Caleb. He goes a little bonkers at times. Josh wants
him to plead temporary insanity."

"He'd be crazy not to."

We both laughed.

I cleared my throat. "So, dear, how did he kill
her?"

"You don't want to know, Mama."

"Yes, I do. I was supposed to take the blame,
wasn't I? Tell me how I was supposed to have
done it."

Charlie looked away. "Caleb, Mama, not you.
He poisoned her."

"How?"

"She had a heart condition, you know."

"No, I didn't."

"Yeah, well, she did. Apparently she got a little
upset at you, and kicked you out. Right?"

"Yes, but what does that have to do with poison?"

"After she kicked you out, she asked Caleb for
one of her pills—she took them all the time—only
this time he gave her a pill of his own. The idea
was to tell the cops that you'd given it to her."

"What kind of pill?"

Charlie took the last slice of pizza. Motherly
spittle didn't seem to bother him.

"I don't know. Josh didn't say. Only that it was
supposed to work right away, only it didn't. So
Caleb broke her neck."

"What?" I couldn't believe I'd heard right.

"He was in the marines, see. He knew how to

kill a man with his bare hands. An old woman was a piece of cake."

"That's horrible!" My mind was racing. It was horrible in more ways than one. If I hadn't upset the Widow Saunders, she wouldn't have felt the need for a pill, and Caleb wouldn't have had the opportunity to carry out his plan.

"Yeah, that's pretty awful, isn't it. But Josh thinks because his brother confessed right away, that they'll take it easier on him. Is that true?"

"I don't know." I stared at the ice in the bottom of my paper cup as my horror turned to anger. Surely investigator Sharp had known about the broken neck. The woman was irritating, but not an idiot. She must have realized that my hands were practically incapable of breaking a wishbone. Apparently she'd been trying to terrify me into a confession regarding Tweetie.

"Mama, what are you thinking about?" Charlie's eyes are blue like his father's, but not as blue as Greg's.

"Nothing, dear."

"Mama, I need to talk to Daddy."

"On Caleb's behalf?" I confess that his desire irked me. While I do want my children to be happy on their own terms, a small—no, make that a large—part of me would rather that their terms didn't include a timber snake.

Charlie shook his head. "Nah, not about Caleb. About Tweetie. I know it's got to hurt Daddy something awful."

I smiled. "You're a good man, Charlie."

"Do you know what time Daddy gets in?"

I shook my head.

"I'd like to meet his plane," he said quietly.

I nodded. Yes, I'd raised a good man.

"I think Malcolm Biddle would know. You want me to call him?"

"Nah, I think I'll just spend the night at Daddy's. My exam isn't until ten."

We cleared the table and then started our rounds of the mall. It soon became clear, however, that as grown up as my son was, he was still not quite ready to be seen shopping with his mama. I left Charlie at the Gap after slipping him a fistful of bills.

"I love you, Mama," he said and gave me a kiss. Thank heavens there were some things my son would never outgrow.

26

I bought a silk animal print scarf at Dillard's for myself, and then, feeling especially generous, bought similar ones for Mama and Susan. Mama would never wear hers, but it would make a nice donation to the white elephant sale at her church. I thought of buying a tie for Greg, but abandoned that idea in favor of a windbreaker. After all, he was going to be spending the bulk of his time in a shrimp boat out on the ocean.

When I left the mall I had just enough time to keep my date with Greg. This posed something of a dilemma, because Malcolm Biddle's South Park home was hardly out of the way, and swinging by would cost me only an extra five minutes. Charlie had given up too easily on the idea of greeting his father at the airport. Malcolm, I was sure, would be happy to take Charlie along, or at the very least, would give me Buford's itinerary.

I called both Greg and Malcolm, but with mixed results. Malcom's answering machine picked up, which meant he might or might not be there. At Greg's, the phone kept ringing, which meant he was out and had neglected to turn the machine on. I tried Malcolm again.

"Hey there," he said cheerfully, "what can I do for you?"

"Malcolm, what time does Buford's plane land, and are you picking him up?"

"I offered to, Abby, but he's coming at one thirty-five in the morning and I have a court case tomorrow at eight. Real nasty divorce. Lots of money involved. Buford insisted he'd take a cab."

I asked Malcolm which airline it was, since I knew there was no direct service to Charlotte from Japan. Buford would be arriving on U.S. Air via Detroit, he said, and gave me the flight number. I scribbled everything down on the back of a church bulletin that had been knocking about in my purse since Mama dragged me to her church for the midnight service on Christmas Eve.

"Abby, you thinking of going out there by yourself?"

"No, it's for Charlie. He misses his daddy."

"Tell him to be careful. That's when drunks rule the highway."

I thanked Malcolm, looked at my watch, and panicked. I was supposed to be at Greg's in fifteen minutes. Greg has teased me before about sometimes being late—it is *not* a habit, mind you—and once said he always cuts me a margin of at least half an hour. That would explain why he wasn't even home. But even with an extra thirty minutes, there was no way I was going to find Charlie in the mall and get there in time.

"Think, Abby," I admonished myself. "Think, damn it!"

I pulled into Buford and Tweetie's driveway with just enough time left on my margin to slip the church bulletin under the kitchen door. I knew that was the door Charlie would use, because folks in the South reserve the front door for company.

It was strange being there. When Buford and I bought the house, the neighborhood was only a couple of years old and sparsely landscaped. But now, with our first frost yet to come, it was lush and leafy. A suburban woods. The crape myrtle to the left of the garage had been no taller than I when I planted it that first year. Tonight it towered above the roof. When first installed, the laurel oaks on the front lawn had had trunks as thick as broom handles. Now they were broader than my chest.

I got out of the car, pretending just for a moment that I was still Mrs. Buford Timberlake—still as happy as I had imagined I was during the first years of our marriage. I might be home from the mall, or I might have just returned from a volunteer stint in the hospital gift shop. Either way, Buford would be inside reading the paper, and there would be a vodka martini waiting for me. Three olives.

The curved flagstone path from the driveway to the kitchen door marked the border of my old herb garden, and it was seeing it again that brought me back to reality. Mrs. Abigail Timberlake would not have let it go to pot. The rosemary bush was way out of hand, a clear indication to me that Tweetie had not been a fan of Mediterranean cooking. The bay tree had either died or been removed, which was understandable because it would have gotten too large. There were no annual herbs, of course; that would have required planting on Tweetie's part. The dominant plant, save for the rosemary, was the perennial catnip I'd planted the day we brought Dmitri home from the pound. In just six years it had virtually taken over the little plot, escaping to fill in the spaces between stones, and even colonizing patches of the main yard itself. One couldn't walk up to the kitchen door now without wading through the stuff.

"Dmitri's going to go bonkers when I get back to Mama's," I muttered aloud. "He's going to roll around on my shoes like a crazed maniac—that's it! I know who killed Tweetie!" It was a wonder the dead woman herself didn't hear me.

Then it really hit me. The knowledge of the blond bimbo's killer was so overwhelming, it literally took my breath away. I sank to the sidewalk and, sitting among the crushed fragrant leaves of mint, tried to gather my thoughts. Of course it had to be him. He had a key to Buford's and Tweetie's house, didn't he? And he was young enough, and strong enough, to wear a suit of armor.

Besides, it was catnip that had made a tom fool out of Dmitri the night before. The killer, dressed in the seventeenth-century cuirass, had walked down this very path, the herbs whipping against the armor with every move, leaving behind their pungent oils. When the suit was stashed beneath my bed, some of the oil must have rubbed off and scented the carpet.

I struggled to my feet, the jungle of mint threatening to pull me down, like the seaweed clump I'd once found myself tangled in while swimming in the Caribbean. Having a sprained ankle only added to the problem. Then adrenaline kicked in and I thrashed my way back to the car. There was only one way to catch a man as clever and diabolical as that, and I knew just how to do it. It was back to Plan A.

The killer stood in the doorway, blocking my view of his foyer. "Abby?"

"Is C. J. here?"

He blinked in surprise. "No."

"Where is she?"

"I haven't the slightest idea."

"Why not? You two were certainly hitting it off. You could have cut the pheromones with a knife."

He didn't even bother to smile. "Yeah, I was attracted to her—at first. But the woman's nuts, you know that?"

"She's a bagel short of a dozen," I agreed.

He stepped back and started to close the door. "Sorry I couldn't help you."

"Wait! We need to talk."

"You want to come in?"

"No thanks. Here is fine." The tiny recorder buried in my bosom was doing its job. It had better be.

"So what do you want to talk about, Abby?"

"I just want to tell you how impressed I am. You actually had me convinced that you'd turned a new leaf."

"I'm afraid I don't know what you're talking about."

"You apologized to me at the Rob-Bobs' for all the times you've hit on me. Very good, Malcolm. And that bit about your wife dumping you, and not the other way around. Stick to the truth, good liars always say. Just mix up things a little, right? Well, you did that beautifully. And that promise to help me find a contractor who could remodel my bedroom so I'd never recognize the murder scene—why, that was a touch of brilliance!"

He smiled. "It was, wasn't it?"

"Oh yes. But the pièce de résistance was when you called during the party to ask if Tweetie was there. That was beyond brilliant. Where did you call from, dear? The next room?"

"I was upstairs in your john, taking a whiz," he said with a grin. "Aren't cell phones nifty?"

"You're scum, you know that? You're worse than scum. You're what's left in the bottom of the garbage truck after it's dumped its load. You're ooooze." I let the word dribble slowly from my lips. "You make me sick. Well, let me tell you something, buster. You're not getting away with Tweetie's murder. I've already told the cops what I've suspected, and that I'm here. So you may just as well give it up. Just tell me one thing—why did you do it?"

I should have remembered that ooze is not a stable substance. I'd been careful to stand well out of Malcolm Biddle's reach, but during my harangue he'd somehow managed to slide over to one side without me noticing. There must have been a console near the door, because the next thing I knew, I was staring into the barrel of revolver.

"Come on in," he said with a triumphant smirk and a wave of the gun. "It's getting a little chilly out there, and I don't want to have to turn the furnace on just yet. Just make sure you leave your purse outside."

An expletive escaped my well-bred lips. I had indeed told the cops what I suspected—well, I'd left a message on Greg's machine—but Malcolm's response wasn't at all what I'd counted on. Buford's junior law partner was supposed to realize that the gig was up. And just as he confessed to everything, the police were supposed to tear up the driveway, their sirens wailing. Now I can see that it was a bit naive on my part, but I am a child of the TV generation. The criminal is always apprehended just in the nick of time.

But while I may be naive, I'm not totally stupid. I had more than just the pepper spray with me this time. I had Amy.

Amy is Buford's gun—don't ask me why he named it that—which he keeps in the nightstand beside his bed. Buford had the gun the entire time we were married, and it was the cause of many fights, especially after the children were born. I demanded that Amy be at least banished to a locked drawer, or the upper reaches of his closet, but my rock-headed ex refused. Amy was for protection, he claimed, and she couldn't do the job in a hatbox on a shelf.

This evening was the first time Amy had ever been pressed into service, but alas, the old gal was in my purse, along with a million and one other things. I fumbled for her, but got my hairbrush instead.

Malcolm laughed. "Drop your purse right there on the steps."

"But it's patent leather," I wailed. "It'll get scraped."

I started edging back down the steps. There were only three of them. Then there was only twenty feet of sidewalk until I reached my car. And then . . .

He released the safety. "Suit yourself, but don't think I won't shoot you. This model is remarkably quiet. The neighbors will think it's just a car backfiring—assuming they even hear it. The couple next door are deaf as posts, and the people across the street are never sober enough to pay attention."

"Don't mind if I do," I said as I dropped my purse and stepped over the threshold. At this point sarcasm was my only weapon. It may not have been much of a tool to wield against him, but it kept me from turning into jelly.

I know, I know. The conventional wisdom is to never allow a gunman to take you into his private domain, be it a car or a house. Most folks couldn't hit the side of a barn with a handgun, and running from your assailant in a zigzag fashion is probably good advice. If you have two good ankles.

Malcolm stepped aside to let me pass, and I noticed with disgust that he had surprisingly good taste in decorating. Somebody had, at any rate. I expected to see a Hugh-Hefner-meets-Arnold-Schwarzenegger thing going on, lots of leather and touches of black lace here and there. Instead, I saw a room with a clean design. One extraordinarily large Persian carpet—probably Joshagan, and probably early nineteenth century—dominated the room, and from it all the colors had been taken and put to good effect. Blue, brown, ivory, it was definitely a man's room, but it didn't knock you over with testosterone.

"Nice place you have here," I said. "Too bad you won't be seeing it for, oh, let's see, twenty years at least. No, better make that the rest of your life." I shook my head. "Pity that you don't look good in stripes. You've got just a touch too much of a waist going on. Still, there might be somebody there who finds you attractive. How would you feel about a girlfriend named Bruce?"

Malcolm laughed. "I've always liked your spunk, Abby."

"Enough to put down your gun and let me go?"

"I'm afraid not. I've got big plans for you. Would you like to hear them?"

27

"If I may sit." Both my ankle and head were throbbing.

"Be my guest." He waved the gun at a contemporary armchair upholstered in cocoa-brown with navy piping. It looked really good with that rug.

I climbed into the chair, sighing with relief as the pain began to drain from my ankle. "Okay, tell me everything."

He sat on a cream-colored sofa right next to me. It was a struggle not to smile with satisfaction. With any luck the recorder in my bra would pick up everything.

"You see, Abby, your timing was perfect."

"*My* timing?"

"Throwing a costume party while Buford was on a trip to Japan."

"That was purely coincidental," I wailed.

"You know that, and I know that, but the police aren't going to know. Look at the facts, Abby— well, the facts as the police will see them. You arranged a costume party the weekend your husband was overseas. Then you went to his house—for which you still have a key—"

"Says who?"

"Give me a break, Abby. Everyone knows that was your dream house, and that the only reason Buford ended up owning it is because he knows how to play the good old boy game. Any reasonable juror would believe you had that key hidden somewhere—maybe in your jewelry box. Besides, even if you didn't keep a key, you could pretty well guess where they hid it. Hmm, front door or back. I wonder which."

"Tweetie was more imaginative than that. She kept it above the lintel. Besides, they would have changed the code for the alarm."

Malcolm grinned. "But they didn't."

"You sure?"

"Quite sure. I'm Buford's junior partner, remember? In his mind, that makes me an errand boy. I have my own damn key. Whenever they're both out of town I pick up the mail, water the plants, you name it. Hell, once I even defrosted the fridge. But where was I? Oh yeah. You'd just broken into Buford and Tweetie's house—"

"I did not!"

"Shhh. It's not polite to interrupt. So, anyway, you stole that suit of armor—one of many Buford recently acquired—lugged it upstairs at your house, and when the party was really cooking— which it was—you killed your ex-husband's wife and stuffed her in that suit. You know, the ex-wife who seduced him away from you and those two precious children of yours?"

"If that's the case, what happened to the sheep?"

He scowled. "That damn sheep! I dumped it off in some farmer's pasture, but it shit in my car first."

"Serves you right."

"Spunky, like I said. Well, back to our little scenario. So you killed Tweetie—"

"*How?* How did I supposedly kill Tweetie?"

"Oh, I guess they haven't told you yet. It was cyanide."

"Ha! Right! Like I have access to cyanide."

"Actually you do. That cherry laurel in your backyard contains cyanide."

"What cherry laurel?"

"That tree you made Tweetie tie her sheep to."

"But I didn't even know it was a cherry laurel. I sure as heck didn't know it contained cyanide."

"That's the breaks. What matters is that the police will think you knew. They'll also think that you planned to get your best friend drunk so she could find the body. Maybe even take the blame."

I was up on my good foot. "That's preposterous!"

"Yeah, maybe it is. After all, it was Buford you were trying to incriminate. Everyone knows they'd been having their problems lately—"

"They had?"

He laughed. "Abby, you're so out of it."

"That may be, but I'm not a cold-blooded killer."

"But are you cold-blooded?"

"I beg your pardon?"

Malcolm laughed again, yawned, and stretched, the gun waving wildly at the ceiling. Had it not been for my game foot, I would have lunged at him, kicked him in the crotch, and maybe gotten the gun. Or I would have taken my chances by making a beeline for the door. Instead, all I could do was watch helplessly while the idiot put his chandelier into jeopardy. The worst of it, I guess, was that he didn't take me seriously.

"Do you like to swim, Abby?"

The light bulb inside my head clicked on. "What's with the riddles, Malcolm?"

I glanced surreptitiously around the room, trying to find something to use as a weapon. My business prevents me from watching much daytime TV, but I'd watched Oprah enough times on my days off to learn that the two best ways to physically disable a man are to kick him in the groin or hit him on the nose. Given the length of my legs, and the fact that one of them was game, I would have to go for the nose. A vase would do it. So would a nice heavy ashtray.

Malcolm didn't seem to notice my wandering eyes. "I'm giving you clues, Abby. It's up to you to guess the riddle."

My eyes lit, just for a second, on the fireplace tools. With a poker I could deliver a nice hard jab to the Biddle family jewels. I might even be able to blind him in one eye. Either way, I'd have enough time to reach the door or call 911.

"What a lovely mantel," I said, and began hobbling toward it.

"Sit down, Abby."

"That looks like white Italian marble," I said, making steady, but slow, progress. "Possibly from Carrara. Is it real, or simulated?"

I never got an answer. Instead, the light bulb inside my head went out, and I took an involuntary nap.

There is, believe it or not, an advantage to being conked over the head with the butt of a revolver. If one's noggin hurts bad enough, a sprained ankle becomes only a minor inconvenience.

I've always been of the opinion that wounds to the head are the most painful, simply because of their proximity to the brain. It is hard to mentally isolate one's head, when that's where one effectively lives. Injury to trunk, I've reasoned, is the second most painful, followed by injury to the arms and legs, and finally the extremities. Now I had a chance to put my theory to the test, and I am delighted to report that, at least in my case, I was right. My head felt like it was going to explode, whereas I could barely feel my ankle.

The light bulb remained out; for all I knew it may even have been broken. I couldn't see a thing. I tried opening and shutting my eyes, but that didn't help. Perhaps I'd been blindfolded. I tried reaching for my face, but discovered I couldn't raise my arm. I tried the other arm and got the same lack of results. I tried my feet. They, too, were immobile. I had the strange sensation of being wrapped in metal. Cold metal.

Was it possible I'd been buried alive? Was it the sides of the coffin I was feeling? But wait a minute, weren't coffins lined with satin or other soft materials? Unless that was all for show, and after the mourners left the graveside, the cemetery workers dumped you into a plain metal container, an expanded version of a safety deposit box.

No, I remembered reading somewhere that casket linings served a distinct purpose; sopping up bodily fluids once decomposition set in. But still, I could be dead. All that business about the tunnel and moving toward the light was only conjecture, wasn't it? Sure, lots of folks claim to have had that experience, but none of them ever stayed. Maybe if you were *really* dead, it felt like being encased in cold metal. At least for a while.

But what about a coma? I'd read that folks in comas can hear everything, even if they can't respond, and I was suddenly hearing things. At first it was just the throbbing inside my head, but slowly I began to discern a low whine coming from outside my metal tomb, and then finally a muffled voice.

I am not a particularly religious woman in the conventional sense, but I definitely believe in God. I decided to take no chances.

"Is that you, Lord?" I asked.

There was a screech of metal alongside both ears

and I finally saw the light. In that instant I realized that I was neither dead nor in a coma. I was encased in a suit of armor.

Malcom Biddle's face loomed over the open visor. Above him I saw stars. Real stars.

"Like your new outfit, Abby?"

"Where the hell am I, and why am I dressed like this?"

He sighed. "You're not very good with riddles. I asked you before if you like to swim."

"I don't," I said. It was true. Buford and I had courted at the water park in Fort Mill, and ever since our divorce I'd been soured on the idea of swimming.

"That's okay, because you're not going to swim. You're going to sink straight to the bottom." He laughed nervously. "That's what I'd do if I fell in. Never learned to swim."

I was lying in the bottom of what appeared to be a bass boat. I struggled to sit. It was possible to move, after all, but it took great effort. Not only did I have the weight of the armor to deal with, but the fact that it hadn't been properly oiled in years. Perhaps centuries.

The sheer weight of the armor made sitting unaided difficult, but I managed to scoot sideways so that I was propped against the boat's side. The small vessel listed precariously.

"How do you like your suit, Abby? It's German. Sixteenth century. As long as I was going to swipe one from Buford, I thought I might as well make it two. Little did I know it would come in so handy."

I only glanced at the armor. "Where the hell are we?"

"Such language, Abby. Still, I suppose you have a right to know, since this is going to be your last resting place. Remember Buford's fishing cabin on Lake Norman?"

"The one that should have at least been mine in the divorce?"

"That's the one. Well, we're in Buford's boat about fifty yards offshore. If I remember correctly, there's a nice little channel, which makes this about the deepest spot around. I'm going to leave the visor open, so that by the time they find you—assuming anyone ever does—the fishes will have done their job. Should make for some mighty big bass come spring."

"You'll never get away with it!"

"Oh yes I will. It's Buford who won't. Sooner or later he'll be charged with both your and Tweetie's deaths. Hmm, I know I'm only a divorce lawyer, but perhaps I can volunteer to defend him."

"Don't be stupid. Buford was in Japan when Tweetie died."

"No he wasn't."

"He called me from there."

Malcolm laughed. "The man's an idiot. Deserved to have his wife run around on him. Buford called you from his new little love nest down in Hilton Head."

"South Carolina?"

"Is there another?"

"But I heard Japanese announcements in the background and—"

"Buford has a tape, Abby. Actually he has several tapes. He can—or should I say could—call Tweetie from virtually every corner of the world. But he was still in Hilton Head."

"But she was his wife! He'd have flown back immediately."

"Would he have?"

The answer, alas, was no. Any man who did what Buford did to me was capable of just about anything. But not murder. It's *not* that the man had too much heart, it was just that he lacked the stomach.

"You'll still never get away with it," I said.

"The hell I won't. And speaking of which, I'd say it was about time you visited it, don't you? It's starting to get a mite light over there in the east. And you know how early fishermen get up."

"Very. There's probably someone watching you right now."

Malcolm stood in the small boat. He was wearing a Charlotte Panthers jacket, and from the right pocket he took that nasty revolver.

"Up," he ordered.

I sat, as still as a bronze statue.

"I'll shoot, Abby. The garniture you're wearing doesn't have a proof mark. The bullet could go right through it."

"Or not. At this range it could just as well ricochet and kill you. Then who'd be feeding the fishes?"

Malcolm pondered that scenario for a moment, before returning the gun to his pocket. Then he charged at me. I can only assume his intent was to take me by surprise and hoist me out of the boat.

But during his moment of contemplation, I'd been doing some thinking of my own. It would take a monumental effort on my part, but one good move was all that was needed. And one good move I gave him. When Malcolm got within reach, I concentrated all my energy into my good leg, and managed to raise it about six inches.

Malcolm tripped and went flying over the bow. Then true to his word, he sank straight to the bottom of Lake Norman. At least I never saw him again.

28

"I still can't believe you're moving to Charleston," Wynnell said as she adjusted my veil for the umpteenth time.

"And I still can't believe Mama agreed to move so readily."

A tug on my hem reminded me that my petite progenitress was still in the bride's changing room. In fact, she was down on her knees sewing a black thread into an otherwise white dress. There had been a bitter battle about the appropriateness of a mother of two walking down the aisle in the color traditionally reserved for virgins. I'd like to think of our compromise as more of a victory for me, but I knew Mama was taking tremendous pleasure in her task. If I didn't keep an eye on her, she was going to have the entire skirt bordered in black before it was time for me to make my grand entrance.

"I didn't need convincing," the crafty seamstress said. "I've always loved Charleston. Abby should have known that. Besides, it's only three hours from here. My friends can visit me anytime."

I thought about having a steady stream of Mama's friends underfoot. "Or you can come back here and visit them," I said not unkindly.

"Don't be silly, Abby. You said there'd be a guest room."

"Yes, but it might be occupied sometimes."

I was thinking of my own friends; Wynnell, C. J., and the Rob-Bobs. The first two I would miss horribly. My daughter Susan had been unable to return from Europe on such short notice, so Wynnell was my matron of honor. She was also my very best friend. As for C. J.—well, she grew on you, not unlike a toenail fungus. I don't mean that in a bad way, of course. It's just that by the time you really noticed that she was part of your life, she'd already been under the surface of things for a long time. And like a toenail fungus, I had the feeling she wasn't going to be that easy to get rid of.

As for the Rob-Bobs, much to my shock, they had announced that they were also considering a move to Charleston. The men were still undecided, but had been toying with the idea for almost year. At first I'd been angry that they hadn't confided in me, but then I realized their silence was in keeping with who they were. Both Rob Goldburg and Bob Steuben are perfectionists—Bob more so than Rob. Until it was a done deal, nobody was going to know. It was only my action that prompted them to reveal the possibility.

Wynnell must have been reading my mind. "I'm going to miss you terribly," she said, and gave me a big hug. Unfortunately her left eyebrow snagged on my veil and she had to readjust it yet again. My veil, not the eyebrow.

C. J., who had insisted on being my flower girl, despite her advanced age, sighed. "Charlotte's not going to be the same without you, Abby, so I've been thinking about going back to Shelby."

"But why? Your business is doing gangbusters."

"That's just it. If you can let Irene run your shop, then I can find someone to run mine. Granny Ledbetter's been after me to help her start a business, and this might just be the time for it."

Apparently Mama thought the black thread was not enough punishment. "What kind of business, dear?"

"It's called Bungee Munchies."

"I beg your pardon?"

"You see, in the summertime a lot of people go bungee jumping in the mountains west of Shelby. Only thing is, they can't eat anytime close to when they jump because it gets kinda messy. But Granny's been experimenting and she's come up with a kind of granola they can eat and still keep it down."

"What kind is that?"

I gave Mama a sharp kick with the toe of my white bridal pump. With all the stiff crinolines in the way I'm sure she barely felt it.

C. J., who was studying the rose petals in her basket, pretended not to hear.

"Well, C. J.?" Mama demanded.

The big gal squirmed. "I promised Granny I'd

keep the recipe a secret. All I can say is that it's got glue in it."

We groaned.

"But it tastes really good," C. J. said defensively. "And our slogan is going to be *What Goes Down, Stays Down.*"

"If you can get it down in the first place," I said wryly.

"Oh, no problem, because—"

Fortunately there was a light tap on the door, and a second later it opened. Charlie stuck his head in, and when he saw me resplendent in my white gown—the one I should have worn at my first wedding—his face lit up.

"You ready, Mama? Greg's standing up by the altar waiting, and I think the organist is about to start."

I smiled at the young man who was going to give me away. "I'm more than ready."

"But I'm not done," Mama wailed.

"You better take your seat, Mama," I said, "or you'll miss the procession."

Mama fled, leaving her sewing basket behind.

One would think that my matron of honor would notice that Mama had left the needle embedded in my hem, but she didn't. As I walked down the aisle to the man I loved, I trailed a long black thread that grew progressively longer, until it pulled off the spool altogether.

But don't be misled into thinking the black thread was an ominous sign. Greg and I are still living happily ever after. In Charleston.

DEN OF ANTIQUITY MYSTERIES

by
TAMAR MYERS

LARCENY AND OLD LACE
0-380-78239-1/$5.99 US/$7.99 Can

As owner of the Den of Antiquity, Abigail Timberlake
is accustomed to navigating the cutthroat world of rival
dealers at flea markets and auctions. But she never thought
she'd be putting her expertise in mayhem and detection to
other use—until her aunt was found murdered . . .

GILT BY ASSOCIATION
0-380-78237-5/$6.50 US/$8.50 Can

THE MING AND I
0-380-79255-9/$5.99 US/$7.99 Can

SO FAUX, SO GOOD
0-380-79254-0/$6.50 US/$8.99 Can

BAROQUE AND DESPERATE
0-380-80225-2/$6.50 US/$8.99 Can

ESTATE OF MIND
0-380-80227-9/$6.50 US/$8.99 Can

A PENNY URNED
0-380-81189-8/$6.50 US/$8.99 Can

NIGHTMARE IN SHINING ARMOR
0-380-81191-X/$6.50 US/$8.99 Can

Discover Murder and Mayhem with

⤳ Southern Sisters Mysteries ⤳

by

ANNE GEORGE

MURDER ON A GIRLS' NIGHT OUT
0-380-78086-0/$6.50 US/$8.99 Can
Agatha Award winner for Best First Mystery Novel

MURDER ON A BAD HAIR DAY
0-380-78087-9/$6.50 US/$8.99 Can

MURDER RUNS IN THE FAMILY
0-380-78449-1/$6.50 US/$8.99 Can

MURDER MAKES WAVES
0-380-78450-5/$6.50 US/$8.99 Can

MURDER GETS A LIFE
0-380-79366-0/$6.50 US/$8.99 Can

MURDER SHOOTS THE BULL
0-380-80149-3/$6.50 US/$8.99 Can

MURDER CARRIES A TORCH
0-380-80938-9/$6.50 US/$8.99 Can

Murder Is on the Menu
at the Hillside Manor Inn
Bed-and-Breakfast Mysteries by
MARY DAHEIM
featuring Judith McMonigle Flynn